SARA'S ANGEL

Sharon Sala

D0048059

A KISMET™ Romance

METEOR PUBLISHING CORPORATION

Bensalem, Pennsylvania

For Kathryn, my inspiration

and

for Iris, who believed in me beyond a mother's pride
and encouraged me to follow my dreams.

SHARON SALA

Sharon lives with Bill, her husband of twenty-five
years, on a farm north of Prague, Oklahoma. One of
her greatest satisfactions has been seeing her son,
Christopher, and daughter, Kathryn, grow to matu-
rity and choose wonderful partners in life as Sharon
did. She's sandwiched a lot of living in between
working as a floral designer, an insurance representa-
tive, a school secretary, a saleslady, even serving as
a court clerk. But all her life she's been a dreamer.
She swears nothing is more satisfying than to give
life to the characters in her mind, then sharing them
with people who love to read.

Printed in the United States of America.

ONE

Mackenzie Hawk watched in silence as the only person he had ever loved was buried beneath six feet of the driest, rock-hard earth in Oklahoma. It was oddly fitting that Old Woman's final resting place was where she had existed in life; between a rock and a hard place.

Hawk felt as if he was being pulled inside out and took a swallow of the cold November air. *How do I live with this emptiness?*

Mother, grandmother, friend. Nona Hawk, Old Woman to her Kiowa kinsmen, had gladly filled all those needs in Mackenzie Hawk's life, and now there was no one. At the age of thirty-seven, for the first time in a life filled with hardship and denial, he was afraid.

Drops of rain began to fall in sparse, scattered patterns, dotting the cold, dry ground and his heavy sheepskin coat with near-freezing bites. Hawk shivered, suddenly aware of the lowering temperature and the misery the few mourners must be experiencing by waiting to speak with him. Slowly he turned from the grave, reluctant to face the old friends who had also braved the harsh, winter winds on the Kiamichi Mountains to bid a final farewell to Old Woman. Hawk suffered the mumbled condolences and handshakes of sympathy in stoic silence. There would be no public display of grief from the big Indian for the mourners to enjoy. Soon they began drifting back to their vehicles, suddenly anxious to get off the mountain before they were stranded by an early winter storm.

Hawk turned back to his silent vigil beside Old Woman's grave. The clods of dirt and rock seemed too harsh a blanket for a final resting place, but he had done as she wished. Old Woman did not want to leave the Kiamichi, not even in death. And so he stood, head bent into the cold winds, unaware a visitor still lingered.

Startled to hear footsteps behind him, Hawk spun about sharply, sending a small plume of dust upwards, coating his pant legs, before it came to rest on the soft, brown leather of his boots. Surprise lifted the deep timbre of his voice as he acknowledged the man's presence.

"Roger! I didn't know you were here."

Hawk's pleasure and surprise at seeing his old friend echoed in the deep, husky growl of his voice. Memories of their years together as partners in the Company came rushing back. All the dangerous assignments, the narrow escapes, the simple joy of awakening to a new day still able to draw a deep breath . . . even Marla's laughter.

Shock stopped the flow of his memories. Hawk shuddered, took a deep mouthful of air, and then nearly groaned aloud at the pain as the cold invaded his inflated lungs. He welcomed the pain. Remembering Marla—and the lies—at a time like this seemed obscene in the face of Old Woman's love and devotion to Hawk, the half-breed baby no one had wanted.

Hawk shrugged and frowned, burying the image of Marla's dark dancing eyes, clouds of black hair, and pouting lips back from wherever it had escaped.

Roger sighed at the frown on Hawk's face. He sensed what his appearance must have caused, what memories he had probably evoked. He knew his friend and ex-partner all too well. The big taciturn man rarely let anyone into his life. And then the one time he had let down his guard to love and trust, a woman's deception had quickly destroyed what might have grown . . . a little faith in the human race. Unfortunately, the only woman Hawk had loved unconditionally and who might have been able to bring Hawk to trust again, lay under six feet of fresh dirt and rocks. Roger suspected Hawk had buried his faith and trust with her.

"Hawk, I'm really sorry about Old Woman. You should have let me know. I would have come sooner."

"Sorry," Hawk said and wearily rubbed his hand across his eyes, squinting against the tiny bits of frozen rain that bit into his cheeks. "How did you find out?"

"The Company," Roger answered. "You know how far-reaching the tentacles of Uncle Sam are."

Roger Beaudry watched a frown dig furrows in Hawk's forehead at the mention of the Company. He knew being sent to Hawk at a time like this was a mistake, but his orders were clear. He had to ask. He looked long and hard at his old friend as tiny shards of sleet fell like frozen tears into Hawk's shaggy pelt of black hair. If he had to describe him, the words *magnificent animal* would have been the first to come to mind. Hawk was tall and lean, with sharply-chiseled features and a hard, hungry look about his eyes. Those cold, jade-green eyes were the unknown legacy that set him apart from his Indian kinsmen. Mackenzie Hawk was indeed a man to be reckoned with.

Roger shuffled his feet and stuffed his numb fingers into his coat pockets.

"Damn, the wind is cold up here. What do you say we go somewhere warm and talk, okay, Hawk?"

Hawk's mouth compressed into a thin, hard line. He watched Roger flush, unable to meet his eyes.

"I doubt we have anything to talk about," Hawk answered.

"The Colonel sends his regrets," Roger mumbled, aware he had already bungled this assignment, but determined to say his piece before he was ordered off the mountain.

"I wasn't aware the Colonel had ever regretted anything in his life," Hawk said, a hard, angry note in his voice.

Roger knew Hawk's bitterness was justified. Nearly two years ago, while Hawk still worked for the Company, and one of the few times he and Roger had not worked as partners, Hawk had inadvertently become an expendable factor in a Drug Enforcement Agency operation. The Colonel's decision to sacrifice Hawk's cover just to find the person responsible for leaking information about Company operations did not agree with Hawk's priorities. He had no intention of being anybody's sacrificial lamb, not even a government lamb. In spite of them all, he had survived.

However, to the Colonel's dismay, Hawk handed him his badge, a government-issue handgun, and gave him a look he still had nightmares about, leaving the Colonel with no further doubts about Hawk's opinion of him, Company policies, or the DEA. Hawk had walked out and never once regretted the decision.

"He wants you to come in and just talk," Roger said, but he was speaking to air. Hawk was already walking into the timberline at the edge of the clearing.

"Hawk! What do you want me to tell him?" Roger

called, but was silenced by the flash of green fire he saw in Hawk's eyes as he looked back. Even at that distance the meaning was clear.

Roger shrugged, pulled his collar up about his ears, and headed toward his car.

"I'm getting off this cold, hellhole of a mountain," he muttered. "I told the Colonel from the start this would be a wasted trip."

Plan A had been a farce from the beginning. Now, Roger Beaudry had his own priorities to consider since Hawk's refusal had been voiced. If what Roger feared was true, because of the men they were after, his own family was already in danger. It was time to go to Plan B.

Soon, there was no one and nothing left in the mountain clearing except a fresh mound of dirt and rocks that was slowly being covered by a glistening blanket of sleet and snow.

High on the mountain, a strong gust of wind pushed against the fortress of Hawk's two-story log cabin, and the lonely sound echoed within the depths of his soul. The big, grey dog resting by the fireplace looked up with concern and whimpered, seeming to sense his master's loneliness.

"What's the matter, Dog? Aren't you getting enough attention?"

In the weeks since Old Woman's funeral, Hawk had existed in a vacuum. Now, he belonged to no one and he belonged nowhere, except here, on the Kiamichi.

For the first time since her death, Hawk wished Old Woman had wanted the television he tried to give her, and the phone he wanted to install, but no electrical gadgets had been welcome in her world.

His gaze rested lovingly on the polished sheen of cedar-paneled walls, hardwood floors that smelled of beeswax and Old Woman's favorite lemon polish, even the thick, multi-colored rugs of heavy, braided cotton belonged in her world. Unfortunately for Hawk, she no longer had any need for them. She had remained firm about some things, yet had welcomed the modern appliances in her kitchen and liked the comfort and convenience of the central-heating system fueled by the massive fireplace circulating its heat throughout the house. But no TV and no phone.

About the time Old Woman's age made coping alone impossible, and mortality beckoned, she knew it was time to call Hawk home. She summoned her son from his wanderings about the world, working for a government that had been his salvation and then . . . nearly destroyed him.

Though Hawk was not of her flesh, he was part of her heart. All the love and nurturing that was in Nona Hawk had been poured into the tiny baby who was literally dropped into her life.

Awakened from her sleep late one night by loud shouts and a constant pounding on her front door, she cringed in fright as she crept from her bed in search of a flashlight and something to use as a weapon. By the time she gained the courage to open her door, there was no one outside. Breathing a sigh of relief, she quickly scanned the darkness with the tiny beam of light from her flashlight and saw nothing. It was a familiar sound that caught her attention, like the mewling of newborn kittens. She turned her light toward the sound in disgust. It wouldn't have been the first time puppies or the like had been thrust uninvited into her life. Only this time, it was different.

Nona Hawk gasped as her light caught on a shallow basket pushed against the wall of her porch. Surely her eyes were deceiving her. But no . . . it was . . . a baby! A tiny, mere hours old baby, with only a blanket between it and the world, lay waiting for something . . . or someone . . . to make the decision for it between life and death.

The beam of light caught its attention and its unfocused gaze tried to follow the light to the source. Then the baby's tiny mouth crinkled into a grimace and a loud, lusty cry echoed into the darkness and down the Kiamichi Mountain.

Nona's flashlight fell unheeded onto the porch as she bent down and scooped the baby from the basket into her arms. Hurrying inside the cabin to warmth and safety, she walked quickly toward the fireplace, kneeling down to use the glow from the banked flames as light to view her uninvited guest. Laying the baby gently onto the thick, braided rug in front of the fireplace, she used her fingers as well as her eyes to see the baby.

"Such a fine, strong baby," she crooned, feeling the sturdy build of tiny shoulders and arms. The baby kicked at the confines of the blanket about its legs and Nona gently pulled the covers away, intent on finishing her appraisal of the baby. "A man-child," she said, surprise entering her voice. The birth of a baby boy is usually met with much joy within an Indian community. *Why*, she wondered, *was this one not wanted?*

The baby's whimpers silenced and his unfocused gaze turned toward the sound of Nona's voice.

"Ahh, so, so," she muttered to herself, as she saw the startling sheen of the baby's emerald-green gaze. "Well, now, little half-breed, so no one wanted you, did they?"

As if sensing the burden he had been born bearing, the baby's face contorted, and his loud, lusty cry echoed within the walls of her cabin.

"Don't cry, little one," she crooned, gathering him and the blanket gently against her breasts. "No one wanted

Old Woman either. Maybe that is why you came, hunh? What do you think, little man?''

And so it was. The days passed, weeks into months, months into years. Old Woman watched him grow and when it was time, pushed him from the nest with pride and regret. Yet when it had become necessary, Mackenzie Hawk came back to the Kiamichi to stay.

But now he was alone. The money he had saved during his years with the government was considerable. And his investments were sound. Although Mackenzie Hawk did not take many chances with friendships, it seemed everything else he gambled on made money. What he lacked in judgment and trust of people, he put wholeheartedly into his own judgment of a good investment. He was rarely wrong.

Mackenzie Hawk had more money than he knew what to do with, and an accountant who was constantly trying to rectify the situation by tax shelters, more investments, and depreciation.

He had money. What he didn't have was a single, solitary soul who cared, except perhaps his dog. With Old Woman gone, the cabin was as empty as Hawk's heart.

Hawk also knew, although he told himself more than once he didn't care, that staying on the Kiamichi when there was no longer a need was foolish. He was merely prolonging his grief by dwelling on his loss. Old Woman would have been the first to shoo him away.

Hawk sighed and then frowned. Dog whined again. The animal turned his massive head toward the door that was fastened tightly against the night's winter breath. By morning, no matter how highly the fire burned inside, there would be an inch of ice on the windows.

"It's only the wind, boy. It's too cold and too late for visitors.''

But Dog would not be silenced. Finally, exasperated, Hawk went to the door, letting a good thirty degrees of heat out into the night as the full force of the winds nearly took his breath away. For a few seconds, he could hear nothing but the whistle of the wind, yet Dog continued to whine, looking into the darkness. And then Hawk heard it, too. A high-pitched sound, spinning and straining, like an engine racing too fast and too hard.

Where there had been only night, came a single eye of light, hurtling out of the blackness. Hawk grabbed the raised fur on the back of Dog's neck, preventing him from bounding off the porch after the one-eyed demon, and so he settled for a menacing growl of warning instead. The demon began to take on a more recognizable form as it came closer and closer to the light spilling onto the porch from behind Hawk.

Some crazy kid on a big Harley! Hawk thought, and he struggled with his pet's increased agitation.

Just as Hawk feared cycle and rider would not make the curve of his yard, it spun about, throwing dirt and gravel into the maelstrom of winter winds. The light from the open door reflected a matching film of dust and dried mud on black leather and black metal alike. It was obvious the ride had been long and wild.

"I'm looking for Hawk . . . Mackenzie Hawk." The words were muffled by the rider's helmet and slurred, nearly blown away by the winds as the rider swayed drunkenly.

"Dog, stay!" Hawk ordered. He closed the door and stepped out onto the porch. It looked as if some drunk kid was on a joy ride up the Kiamichi, although this stunt was usually reserved for warmer weather.

I better get him inside to sleep it off or he'll probably freeze to death before he sobers up, Hawk thought.

The rider dismounted from the cycle, staggering slightly as though solid ground were a strange phenomenon. Hawk grabbed at the leather-clad arm, intending to hasten them both inside to warmth when the rider crumpled to the ground.

"Damn!" Hawk muttered, and quickly bent down, intent on carrying his uninvited visitor inside. Hard muscles bunched and rippled across his back, straining the soft, flannel fabric of his shirt as he lifted the rider upward into his arms. With a single motion, the rider's head rolled limply against Hawk's arm and the cycle helmet fell off, hit the ground, and bobbed awkwardly about until it came to rest against the porch steps.

Hawk froze and watched the hair spill out of the helmet and over his arms before the wind whipped the long, fiery strands across his neck and face. A woman! Some crazy, redhead had taken the Kiamichi in the dark, at breakneck speed, in the dead of winter.

She has to be crazy, Hawk thought, entering the house. Sidestepping Dog, he kicked the door shut behind him. Hawk carried her closer to the fire and laid her carefully on a long, leather sofa. She sank limply into its depths, her hair in wild abandon, scattering in tangled curls onto the pillows cushioning her head.

Damn! She is so pale and too still, Hawk thought. His heart began to race as he thrust his hand into the fiery tangle of hair about her throat, searching for a pulse. It was like touching satin—cold, white satin. He felt the smallest of tremors at the base of her throat and breathed a quick sigh of relief, but it was obvious she was in distress.

Hypothermia at the very least, maybe frostbite, he thought, quickly scanning her fingertips for telltale signs. "No time to be a gentleman about this," Hawk muttered.

Dog watched in stillness, his dark eyes following his master's every move.

Layer by layer, working swiftly and silently, Hawk stripped the clothing from the woman's body. He threw a heavy woolen blanket over her nudity, left her on the sofa, and once again ordered Dog to stay.

Hypothermia, hypothermia . . . what in hell are the steps for treating hypothermia? This must have been covered in survival training, he thought, hurrying down the long hallway to his bathroom.

Scattered bits of lost knowledge began to surface in Hawk's mind while he knelt by the bathtub and began filling it with water. In an instant, he was back by the fireplace, standing over the still body of his unexpected guest.

"I don't treat all my guests this way, lady. You'll just have to take my word for it," he muttered and leaned over.

Hawk threw aside the blanket cover and once again scooped her into his arms. The bathtub was about half full as he knelt down and carefully lowered her, feet first, into the tub.

She moaned and weakly tried to lift herself from the chilly bath before slipping back to an unconscious state.

"I know, lady, I know. I fell into a creek once in the dead of winter. But you got yourself into this shape, I'm just trying to save your pretty hide," Hawk whispered, and lifted her head higher onto his arm.

An icy wave sloshed over the side of the tub and all the way down the front of Hawk's clothes.

"Damn, that's cold," he groaned, watching the spreading stain on his shirt and down onto his lap. "Hope nothing shrinks permanently, but it sure feels like it did." He shuddered against the chill.

Dog whined softly from the doorway of the bathroom. "We're okay, boy. Go back by the fire."

Hawk kicked the door closed as his furry companion silently obeyed. Over the next hour, Hawk gradually replaced the chilly waters with warmer and warmer temperatures until the woman's body was rosy pink and beads of perspiration lined her upper lip and across her forehead, plastering errant curls damply to her face and neck.

A thick fog of warmth and humidity filled the small room, infiltrating every pore and fiber of Hawk's body and clothes. His muscles ached from the strain and tension of keeping her head from sliding under the water level and her dark auburn curls kept getting tangled in the buttons of his shirt while he held her carefully in his arms.

Her hair sure has a mind of its own, he marveled, unwinding for the umpteenth time an orphan strand of hair from two of his shirt buttons. The colors were dark and rich, blended like the leaves of Indian summer on the Kiamichi Mountains. Deep reds with darker brown undertones fought with gold-shot strands for dominance as it twisted sensuously about.

Hawk slowly replaced the cooling waters with a fresh supply of warm and wondered what would make someone commit a foolhardy act such as this woman had. It was suicide on the mountain at night. The roads were dark and one-laned. Absolutely no light, except moonlight, was able to filter through the trees that bordered the narrow paths.

He leaned back on his heels and expelled a shaky sigh of relief. She seemed to be showing signs of regaining consciousness. Her pulse had steadied and her eyelids fluttered weakly, as she fought against the lethargy the warm water and an exhausted state had induced.

Hawk began to move quickly. He had to get her out of

the tub, dry, and into a bed before she awakened. He didn't know how she would react to waking naked in a tub of warm water with a strange man watching, but he had no intention of finding out.

With one arm still under her neck for support, he leaned over to release the stopper from the tub. Hawk watched the lowering waters slowly reveal the ivory perfection of the woman's long-limbed grace. Now that imminent danger concerning her health had passed, Hawk no longer denied himself the right to a better inspection of his uninvited guest.

Her firmly-toned body hinted at daily workouts and classic, delicate features revealed a beauty that needed no makeup for enhancement. She had a wide, sensuous mouth, a thick brush of eyelashes just darker than her hair, delicately arched brows, and a stubborn jut to her chin that seemed to go naturally with such fiery curls.

She was beautiful . . . and Hawk didn't want her there. The physical perfection of her body and face made Hawk's body react with a persistent ache he did not welcome. Strangers, regardless of beauty, were not his style. He was past the age of indiscriminate encounters, no matter how enticing. And, after Marla's deceit, Hawk didn't trust such beauty. She'd used her looks as a mask to hide behind, and then finally, even her beauty had not been enough to save her.

Distracted from his musing by the woman's increased agitation, he reluctantly smoothed damp ringlets from her forehead. He watched her struggle, unwilling to touch her in any way other than impersonal care. Hawk watched her grimace and flick the delicate rose tip of her tongue slowly across her swollen, wind-chapped lips, and fought the urge to follow in its path. Perspiration pooled and ran unchecked down her cheeks like tears.

"So warm," she whispered, "cold . . . tired . . . freezing. Now, so warm. Heaven."

"No thanks to you, lady," Hawk muttered, as the last of the water emptied down the drain. He wrapped her damp body in a blanket and carried her back to the warmth and comfort of the sofa by the fire.

She sighed and snuggled deeply into the cushiony comfort of her makeshift bed as Hawk covered her gently with extra blankets.

Hawk was struck by how natural this seemed, caring for a woman again, and realized it was probably because of Old Woman. Her last days had been like this for him. Having someone to care for again seemed . . . familiar. He glared accusingly at the young woman as she lay sleeping and resented the emotions she had stirred in his angry heart.

The house was in darkness and the only illumination in the room was from the dying embers of the fire in the massive stone fireplace. Hawk added firewood from the stack on the hearth so the winter chill would not overtake the comfort of the room. All he needed was for her to get pneumonia and then he would be saddled with a stranger for weeks. It was next to impossible to get off the mountain when it snowed, and snow was in the forecast.

Backing up to the flickering warmth, he wearily began to remove his own wet clothing, intent on finally getting some much needed rest. His guest seemed to be holding her own. He was down to a snowy strip of cotton that passed for men's underwear, molding tight, muscular buttocks, a hard, flat stomach, and his bulge of manhood. He spun about, forgetting his nearly nude state, when he heard her speak.

He is so beautiful. A dark god standing in the light. Squinting her eyes weakly against the unaccustomed light of the brightly burning logs, she whispered softly, "I died . . . dear God. I tried so hard. An angel . . . so beautiful . . . must be Heaven. My angel is . . . so beautiful," and her eyelids fluttered, too heavy to stay open.

Hawk knelt swiftly, hoping to catch some clue from her rambling words.

"What's your name, lady?" Hawk asked softly, and grasped her chin, gently turning her face toward his searching gaze.

"Sara . . . name Sara. My angel . . . please help," and her words became incoherent as she again drifted into slumber.

"I'm no angel, lady," Hawk whispered, his calloused thumb gently tracing across her wind-burned lips, lingering unnecessarily on the tiny cleft in her proud chin. "Not anymore. I fell from heaven a long time ago."

She continued to toss and turn, murmuring softly from time to time. Assuring himself she was all right, Hawk gathered his wet clothing from the floor, tossed them on top of the washer in the kitchen, and let Dog in from his nightly prowl. He had started up the stairs to bed when something the woman kept repeating caught his attention.

He stepped away from the bottom stair and walked back to his unwelcome guest. A wary look and then growing anger deepened the green fire in his eyes. His lips thinned and then compressed in fury as he silently absorbed the muttered words.

"Hawk will help. Roger says tell Hawk. Tell my angel . . . Hawk must save Roger. Company . . . trouble." Her words faded into nothing. She turned her head into the softness of the sofa cushions and drifted into a deeper sleep.

A burning log in the fireplace behind Hawk popped,

sending a shower of sparks against the screen. Echoing sparks of fury exploded behind the green fire in his eyes.

"Sonofabitch," he said, looking about wildly for something to throw. The Company wasn't satisfied when I told Roger at Old Woman's funeral I wasn't interested. They had to send some crazy female to get me back. "Well, to hell with the Company," he muttered, "to hell with Roger, and to hell with you, lady. Did they think I was so damn stupid I'd fall for this twice in one lifetime?"

He stood over the unsuspecting woman, naked muscles glowing like burnished teakwood in the firelight, as he clinched and unclinched his fists in frustration.

"I should have let you freeze."

With that bitter epitaph hurled into the darkness, he stomped up the stairway and into the shadows.

Dog whined softly, aware of his master's agitation. He watched him disappear up the stairwell and then looked at the stranger who slept by the fire. Sniffing the old braided rug on the hearth, he turned around two or three times until he was satisfied and claimed his bed.

Soon, the snap of an occasional log as the fire burned into a pocket of sap, and the mournful sound of the winter winds outside the snug walls of the cabin were the only signs of life on the Kiamichi Mountain.

TWO

A hard-rock rhythm bounced the Jimi Hendrix classic "Wild Thing" off the padded walls of the sound studio. The tall, leggy redhead in tight, black leather strutted and pouted in sync until observers were uncertain where the song stopped and the redhead began.

"That's great, baby. Great! This new commercial is gonna sell cars like crazy!"

The voice of the heavyset director standing somewhere behind the heat and blinding lights made Sara wince as she turned her back to the cameras and rolled her hips suggestively.

There's got to be a better way to make a living, Sara thought, and then sighed in relief as she faintly heard someone yell over the din.

"Cut, that's a wrap."

Sara turned to see Morty Sallinger, her manager, threading his way through the people and props with determination, and began mentally preparing herself for the confrontation she knew she would have to endure.

23

"You were fantastic, Sara," her manager wheezed, and ran his beefy fingers suggestively up and down the hot, leather sleeves of her jacket and down the curve of her backside.

"How about dinner tonight? We'll discuss your next assignment. If this spot takes off like I think it will, you're gonna be the hottest thing on video. There won't be enough Wildcats on the showroom floors to keep up with the demand. The car will be as hot as you are. So . . . whadaya say?"

The leer and suggestive manner of Morty made her shudder. With revulsion in every nuance of her body language, she backed casually away from his too familiar manner. After eight years in the business, she was adept at sidestepping such invitations without alienating her future, yet it still left Sara feeling dirty. She resented having to play these games to retain her privacy and personal integrity.

"Now, Morty," Sara said, and bent down to pick up a bulky shoulder bag. She always carried a complete change of clothes and all the necessities for the instant beauty her job required. "You know I have an early shoot tomorrow for that new makeup account. You don't want me to look all puffy-eyed on my close-ups, do you?"

She smiled what she hoped was a congenial smile in his direction. What she'd really like to do was put his beefy hands in buckets of concrete and when it hardened, drop him into the nearest river.

"Oh, Sara," one of the workers called out, "this letter came Special Delivery a couple of hours ago. I signed for it so you wouldn't mess up your take. Hope you don't mind."

"Of course not, Paul. You're a doll."

She waved her thanks to the makeup man who handed her the letter.

Sara was a favorite within the modeling community. In a business where fame was as fleeting as the beauty of the models, and as fickle, Sara was one of the few who had made the transition from ingenue to near-superstar status.

She flopped wearily into one of the numerous folding chairs about the set and tore into the letter. Unaware she was being observed—unaware the contents of the letter were about to set a series of events into motion that would forever change her life.

"Yes, sir! She's still on the set. I've been observing her every move for nearly a week. Say the word, and I'll contain the problem immediately."

The man was nondescript. He'd been hired, as always, to do certain jobs no one else either could, or would, do. And his job, this time, was Sara Beaudry. How he managed to get her was unimportant to his boss. Just get her was the order . . . and he followed orders very well. He blended into the stage crew and media personnel as if he wasn't there. It was his job to be inconspicuous. It was also his job to be thorough. He was very good at his job.

"Sir?" he questioned. The wall phone he was using hung in a darkened corner of the studio, and he continued receiving his orders unobserved.

"Yes, sir, immediately. I'll contain the situation before nightfall." He hung up the phone, his gaze searching the milling crowd on the sound stage, and then smiled slightly to himself as he spotted his . . . job across the room.

Sara was delighted when she realized the letter was from Roger. He was all the family she had. Although their respective occupations prevented them from spending as much time together as they would have liked, they were still very close.

At first glance, Sara thought her brother was playing a joke because the letter made no sense. Then, rereading the odd message, apprehension forced a nearly forgotten warning Roger had given her years ago when he first began working for the government to surface. Something was wrong. Sara was sure of it. Her hands trembled, scanning the brief note for further clues that would assure her she was mistaken. But there were none. Panic weighted her breath and loud, slow heartbeats hammered in her ears as if her blood was too thick to flow. Sara read the note for the third time, memorizing every comma and nuance.

Sara, our holiday plans are blown. Sure sorry. If things don't change soon, looks like I'll be with Mom and Dad for Christmas instead of with you as planned. I hate for you to be alone, although I'm sure you're NOT right now. Why don't you take an extended vacation? You work too hard. I'm sure the rest would do you more good than you know. Once again, sorry. I'll be in touch. Say hello to Big Bird for me. Love, Roger

Sara leaned against the back of the chair and casually stuffed the letter into the depths of her shoulder bag. She ran a shaky hand through the tangled mane the hairdresser had given her for the Wildcat look, mentally deciphering the contents. *Roger was in trouble. His cover was blown. His life was in danger, and if she read him correctly, so was hers.*

Their parents had been dead for seven years. They died in a plane crash on their way to a second honeymoon. If Roger's reference to spending Christmas with them was sincere . . . *dear God,* she thought. And then stifled the panic that threatened. She took a deep breath. This had to look good.

Sara rose, stretched as if working the kinks from her back and legs after the grueling shoot, and looked around. She casually began removing her heavy makeup just as she did everyday after filming was finished. She didn't see anything or anyone suspicious, but she wasn't taking chances. If Roger told her to get to Big Bird, she knew she was in danger. From the few things she remembered Roger saying about his former partner, the man was formidable. Better to have him as an ally than an enemy. If she was in need of a refuge, it would have to be Mackenzie Hawk. There *was* one problem she still faced. Sara only knew one place to look for him. If he was gone from the mountains, then God help her and Roger, because there would be no one else left who could.

It seemed fortune knew Sara needed a diversion. At that moment a section of backdrop was knocked down by a large piece of expensive sound equipment. A furor arose as grips and gaffers scurried about, anxious to assess the damage and correct it so tomorrow's shooting schedule would not be delayed. Sara took advantage of the confusion, slung her bag casually over her shoulder, and walked out the side door.

Her pulse quickened, and her mind raced, frantically discarding one idea after another about how to get out of Dallas unobserved. Sara unlocked the door of her Wildcat. Candy Apple Red was not a color to be overlooked and the manufacturer considered it money well spent to furnish the female version of their Wildcat with one of their mechanical ones. She slid behind the wheel, oblivious to the interior luxury, and shakily jammed the key into the ignition. She fastened her seat belt and adjusted the rearview mirror for an overall view of the parking lot and the studio she had just exited. To the casual observer, it would seem she was merely being a cautious driver.

I made it! she thought and shakily grasped the steering wheel. Unobserved, she left the parking lot and entered the busy mainstream traffic of downtown Dallas. If Roger's warning was valid, she knew her safety was contingent on leaving Texas unnoticed, and that certainly meant she could not drive the Wildcat. She and the car were becoming synonymous. Public transportation was unacceptable, so that left her one fast alternative.

The sun was setting as Sara wheeled into the private underground parking provided by the elaborate security of her condominium complex. She parked the car, exited, and began a quick search of the area. Assuring herself she was still alone, she hurried to the large storage areas provided for the residents, unlocked the one that corresponded with her apartment number, and disappeared into the boxlike structure. In less than a minute, Sara reappeared in the open doorway of the storage room pushing a black, nearly new, Harley Davidson motorcycle. It, like the Wildcat, was a remnant of a modeling assignment.

Thank goodness I had to learn to ride this thing, Sara thought. *Surely, no one will expect me to leave town on a motorcycle.*

In less time than it takes a Texan to say fajita, she was gone. One quick stop at a self-serve station for fuel and she was eastbound out of Dallas on Interstate 30 with the winter sun dying behind her.

"Yes, sir, the Wildcat is in its usual parking space. When it gets dark, I'll make my move. I'll keep you informed."

The man hung up the phone, angry with himself for missing his chance earlier. His boss didn't suffer fools gladly. There couldn't be a second mistake; he didn't have an option. Unfortunately for him, his wait was to be long and fruitless in the lowering temperature of a Dallas December. Sara Beaudry was gone.

An ache had begun while she was asleep that was insinuating itself into her consciousness with a niggling, painful persistence. Sara had been aware once or twice during the night of no longer being on the motorcycle, and of strong arms and a gentle voice. She also was aware of no longer being lost or cold. Beyond that, she was incapable of thinking because there was that sharp, stabbing pain behind her eyelids everytime she moved that sent her floating back into a deep, dreamless oblivion.

It was the smell of coffee that pushed past the pain in her head and pulled her closer and closer to awakening. Sara knew she didn't drink coffee and her mind was struggling with the problem of why she kept smelling something she didn't even buy when the memory of the past few hours flooded back into her consciousness, sweeping aside everything except the unwavering fear and panic she'd felt as her journey to the Kiamichi and Mackenzie Hawk had begun.

Sara moaned, struggled wildly to free herself from the weight of the restricting bedclothes, and with no small effort sat straight up in bed. She was also instantly aware of not knowing where she was or how she had arrived. As she began struggling to focus on her surroundings, she became aware of being on a sofa, not a bed as she had first imagined, and of a menacing figure of a man standing between her and a fire burning in the largest fireplace she'd ever seen.

Hawk watched the woman struggle with confusion and bedcovers, and knew a moment of sharp desire as the blankets slipped down to cradle about her narrow, shapely waist. The emotion only angered him more and painted an even fiercer expression on his face.

Sara blinked rapidly, unaware of her nudity or how much of herself she'd revealed as she sat up. The pain in her head was increasing and the smell of that coffee made her nauseous. She moaned, tried to stand, and only succeeded in nearly falling face first in the tangled covers about her feet.

Hawk muttered a none-too-silent curse as he leaped forward, catching her just before her head hit the floor. He yanked her up rather unceremoniously, roughly shoving the fallen covers back over her shoulders, but Sara was unaware of the byplay. She was too busy trying not to be sick.

"Please," Sara mumbled, barely able to speak for fear of more than words coming out of her mouth. "I'm going to be sick," she finally managed and felt herself propelled down a hallway to, thankfully, a bathroom with mere seconds to spare.

Without saying a word, Sara sank limply onto the closed seat of the commode and let this strange man wipe her face and hands. Swathed in a tangled wad of blankets, she was incapable of moving, yet his gentle ministrations felt oddly familiar. She leaned back against the natural wood paneling, closed her eyes, and let him do whatever it took to make things right.

Hawk rinsed the cloth he was using on her pale face, letting the water run warm through his fingers, and resisted the urge to touch the childlike twist of despair that was shaping her lips. He knew she was trying not to cry because she kept swallowing, as if forcing back whatever emotions were threatening to choke her. A tiny tear squeezed out from under her closed eyelids and down her cheek only to be caught by Hawk's fingers as he carefully washed away her despair.

Sara opened her eyes at his gentle touch and Hawk forgot to move or breathe. And when he finally regained his senses, his breath escaped in a long, angry rush.

Her eyes are nearly gold, he thought, and knew a sudden, inescapable emotion he hadn't experienced since the eve of Old Woman's death. It was fear. The old, unfamiliar emotion brought another unwanted memory to the fore—and that was the deceit of another beautiful woman, and another time he had carefully and methodically buried deep in his soul. Coupled with that and his anger at her presence, Hawk drew back sharply, doubling his fists in frustration at his attraction to this uninvited visitor and let the damp cloth in his hand drip onto the floor as he unconsciously squeezed it dry.

Sara leaned her head back, weakly resting against the wall behind her. For the first time, she allowed herself a look into the face of her rescuer and knew instant relief. She'd found him—Mackenzie Hawk. The few pictures Roger had of him didn't begin to do him justice, but the image of the man was the same. The pictures just hadn't allowed the overpowering presence or barely-leashed energy to show through. Her relief was short-lived as she touched her hand to her midriff and then gasped as she finally discovered her true condition. She didn't have a stitch of clothes on her body. She fairly glowered at the man before her and had to bite the inside of her lip to keep from screaming in rage. How dare he!

"You are Mackenzie Hawk, aren't you?" she asked, forcing back the urge to do something violent to the glaring menace standing so silent and judgmental before her.

"And what if I am . . . Sara . . . or whatever your name is," Hawk growled. "It'll do you no good to be here. You made a trip up this mountain for nothing and you can ride right back down the same way. My answer to the Company was *no* weeks ago, and it's still *no* today. You froze your pretty ass for nothing.''

"I don't know what you're talking about," Sara said, her voice shaking as she stood, "but you have a lot of nerve yelling at me when you waited until I was helpless and then stripped me down to nothing. Did you get a good look?" she asked sarcastically, her voice rising in anger with each uttered word.

"I didn't do it for kicks, lady," Hawk bit back angrily, unable to mask the flush on his cheeks as he rudely answered her accusations. "You were suffering from exposure and were cold as ice. Maybe you would rather I'd let you freeze. It sure as hell would have saved me a lot of grief today if I had." He glared back just as fiercely.

Sara watched the green fire in his eyes flare into a wild, angry heat and knew he spoke the truth. However, it did nothing to help the anger that now stood between them as she continued.

"I thought you were Roger's friend. Roger said you were the only . . .''

"I was . . . am," he corrected, and jammed his hand angrily through his already tousled hair, making him appear more like a fierce warrior than ever. A giant of a man, he paced about the tiny enclosure, dwarfing it and Sara until she felt suffocated from her despair for Roger and Hawk's lack of understanding.

"Roger said you would help me," she persisted, pushing her chin out in a gesture of defiance.

Hawk admired her courage in spite of himself. There she stood, red hair all over the place, wearing nothing but a blanket, and after being as sick as a skunked dog only moments before, she dared to look like some kind of queen.

"The Company sure can pick them," Hawk growled to himself, resisting the urge to brush the tangle of hair away from her tear-filled eyes, knowing full well she wouldn't welcome his touch now.

"Company?" Sara sniffed, puzzled at his constant referral to company business. "What company? The last one I worked for made Wildcats. What does that have to do with you?"

"Wildcats?" Hawk muttered. Now it was his turn to be puzzled.

"Yes," she sighed, "the new car of the 90s."

"Car?"

Sara looked at Hawk in disgust.

"Never mind all that," she ordered and drew a shaky breath. "Are you going to help me or not? Roger is all I have and he said to trust you, so . . ."

Sara shrank back against the wall as Hawk walked toward her, cold, implacable fury in his every word and gesture.

"I'm only going to say this once and then you get back in your leather, back on that Harley, and get off my mountain. I'm not going back to work for the Company, not now, not later, not even if they send me assorted flavors and colors."

"Oh, for Pete's sake," she shouted, and then grabbed her head in pain and frustration. "I don't work for this company you keep talking about, and I'm damn sure not your paid enticement either."

"Then what? . . ." Hawk began, but was cut off by Sara's sharp retort.

"If this company you keep referring to is the same branch of the federal government that Roger works for, then you have it all wrong. I don't work for them. I'm not even certain what Roger does for them. I'm a model, a very successful one, too,'' she muttered. ''At least I was until yesterday when I abandoned my career for this . . . this nightmare.''

Hawk stood silently, judging her story for himself, expecting to poke holes in it with satisfaction, but he could not ignore the fear in her eyes nor her extreme agitation.

''My name is Sara Beaudry,'' she said, and took a deep, shaky breath as she continued. ''Roger is my brother. He's missing.''

Hawk's eyes narrowed, seeing all the nuances of pure fear on her face. Yet this didn't ring true. Roger wouldn't send a woman to get help for himself. And he'd been Roger's partner for four years. He had never heard him mention a sister. There had to be more to this story.

Sara sank limply back to her seat on the commode.

''Couldn't we have this discussion somewhere else?'' she asked, and once again leaned her head weakly against the paneling.

''Are you going to be sick again?'' The big man's gentle voice was nearly her undoing.

''No,'' she muttered, glaring in spite of another tear that escaped from her brimming eyes and ran for its life down her face. Only it disappeared forever when a rough, calloused finger gently ended its foolhardy escape. There was no escape from the Kiamichi Mountain, or from Mackenzie Hawk—not today.

''Okay then, we talk,'' he agreed and shocked Sara as he bent down, lifted her from her throne, covers and all, and once again carried her back to her sofabed by the fireplace.

With as little drama as possible, Sara repeated the events of the past twenty-four hours to Hawk in minute detail, leaving out nothing she thought would be important to her brother's safety. Only after she'd finished her recital did she venture a glance toward Hawk. She managed a silent sigh of relief as she saw some signs of acceptance on his face.

Hawk leaned back in his chair, locked his hands behind his head as he stretched his long, powerful legs out before him.

Sara watched, transfixed in spite of herself at the pure, unadulterated sexuality he wore with no regard for the effect it had on the opposite sex. His next question ended her wild flights of fancy and brought her back to earth with a sarcastic thud. She was still going to have to convince him.

"Where's the letter?" Hawk asked, expecting her to say she'd lost it or left it behind, her answer took him by surprise.

"It's on my bike, I . . . no," Sara muttered to herself and missed the look of disdain on Hawk's face. "No," she continued, "I think I stuffed it in my bag. Is my bag still on the bike? I hope I didn't lose it. I don't have any other clothes," she muttered and couldn't resist one last look of accusation at Hawk with regard to the state of her undress.

Hawk refused to let her words fluster him this time, and remained unbelieving of her earnest response. Instead, he pulled himself up from his seat like a big cat uncoiling from a lazy sleep in the heat of the sun, and silently walked from the room.

Sara pulled the covers up over her shoulders, shielding herself as best she could from the blast of cold air that slipped past the front door as Hawk pulled it shut behind him.

In less time than it took to curse the fates that had

brought her here, Hawk was back, bringing a sharp, pine-scented freshness into the room with him in the form of another cold gust of wind. He plopped a large, bulky bag in her lap and stood beside her elbow without speaking as Sara dug through the contents.

"Here," she announced defiantly, pulling the object of her search from the bag and shoving the letter into Hawk's outstretched hand.

Hawk's eyebrows rose more than slightly at her defiance and he realized again what a handful of woman had been dumped on his doorstep. He ignored the snort of disdain she delicately managed and took the letter over to the window for better light.

Sara was drawn, in spite of herself, to the broad shoulders, taut belly, and lean, narrow hips of his silhouette as he stood before the window. The interest she felt in spite of her anger confused her jumbled thoughts. She was so engrossed in watching him that when he spoke, it startled her. And unconsciously, she let the cover slide from her bare shoulders as she turned to hear his words.

"Are you certain you were not followed?" Hawk asked.

In spite of his initial distrust, he was beginning to realize the seriousness of the situation Sara believed existed. He was also disgusted with Roger for involving him, but knew in all probability Roger felt he could trust no one else with his sister's safety. Hawk believed that much of her story. He paced the floor in front of the fireplace as he awaited her answer.

"About as certain as I can be," Sara answered. "I suppose if anyone was very close behind, they would have found me while I was unconscious. I missed a curve on the way up here. I don't know how long I was out, but I vaguely remember coming to and feeling extremely cold and disoriented."

She brushed a shaky hand carelessly through her hair and winced as she felt a tender area at one side of her temple.

"I guess I'm lucky I didn't go back down the mountain in confusion."

"Unconscious!" Hawk nearly shouted, "What in . . ."

He pivoted toward Sara, alarm and comprehension dawning as some of the symptoms she had exhibited earlier began to make sense.

Sara gasped and yanked the covers as far under her chin as they would go. Hawk was heading toward her with a look on his face she wished she wasn't responsible for. The man definitely made her nervous and she didn't like being out of control.

"My God, lady! Why didn't you tell me sooner? You probably have a concussion as well, and I assumed it was only exhaustion or exposure—something."

Hawk muttered to himself about the monumental stupidity of the redhead lying on his couch as he gently thrust his hands in the hair at her temples.

"I should have suspected earlier when you were sick . . ." and his voice trailed away as he very carefully kneaded her scalp, inch by inch, searching for any further signs of injury.

Something happened when Hawk touched her that Sara didn't expect. She liked it. She didn't think it was such a good idea, but her pulse was overriding her guidance system of good judgment and Sara sighed as she let herself melt at the touch of his fingers kneading carefully and sensuously on her scalp. Sara was mesmerized by the man and the feel of his hands on her body and in her hair. *This man should be declared illegal*, Sara thought. *He is too dangerous and too tempting.*

Hawk glanced down. His eyes locked with Sara's hypnotic stare. He was lost. His hands stilled, forgotten in the spell of her gaze.

Sara's pulse quickened. She nervously flicked the tip of her tongue across her slightly parted lips and watched the green fire in Hawk's eyes flash and deepen with a look she was afraid to interpret.

Hawk's chest tightened, constricting his every breath as his eyes followed the path of her tongue on her lips and fought the urge to bury himself so deep in . . .

"Hawk," Sara whispered.

He had to restrain from accepting her unconscious invitation as the cover slipped dangerously close to the tightly budded tips, teasingly obvious beneath the retreating covers.

Sara reached toward him and Hawk jumped as if he'd been shot.

What in hell am I thinking? Then he knew, mentally answering his own question. *That's what is wrong. I haven't been able to think since she rode in with last night's storm. Dammit, I don't want this.* He stood back and stared at Sara as if she had suddenly grown horns.

"Well, what do you think?" Sara asked, watching Hawk try to focus his thoughts on her question.

"Think?" he muttered, completely lost as to the origin of this discussion. Then he blurted out the only thing he knew that would save his sanity. "I think you better get dressed and then spend the day in bed."

"Get dressed to stay in bed?" *This man is not exhibiting any of the qualities Roger bragged about. I'm beginning to doubt the wisdom of burying myself in the wilds of the Kiamichi Mountains with this man. He can't make up his mind about anything.*

Then, his next words set her mind at ease about incompetence, but her emotions went into overdrive. He left no lingering doubts in Sara's mind.

"If you don't want to spend the rest of your born days in bed—my bed—you damn well better get dressed," he growled.

Hawk turned away from Sara in disgust and jammed his hands into his hip pockets. It seemed to be the only safe place for them at the moment. *Great! I certainly clarified this situation,* he thought.

Sara's eyes widened and she gasped in indignation at his words. He obviously wasn't giving her a choice in the matter and Sara hated ultimatums.

"If you'll excuse me," Sara stated with more dignity than she felt as she held the covers tightly about her nudity. It wasn't her fault the needle on their sex drives was shooting into the danger zone. He had obviously been on this damn mountain alone too long. "I'll just slip into a little something comfortable," she said with sarcasm dripping from every syllable and exited the room with her bag dragging on the floor behind her.

Hawk was appalled at himself and speechless at what he'd just said to a woman he didn't even want here. He started to call her back and try to explain his outburst. However, he stopped himself before he could utter a word. He didn't have an explanation for his actions. He didn't know what had come over him and he intended to do his best to see that whatever it was didn't surface again. He let her leave without saying anything further. He figured he'd already said more than enough.

Sara dug in her shoulder bag, angrily yanking item after item out of the bag and onto the floor and countertop in the bathroom where she'd gone to change. She knew she was making a mess and she knew she was acting childish, but the man made her so mad.

Hawk was leaning against the wall in the hallway, listening to Sara's fit. It didn't sound as if anything was being broken, but she certainly was rearranging space. A tiny smile worked its way into the corner of his mouth. One thing was certain about Sara Beaudry, a man knew where he stood with her. She wasn't very good at hiding her feelings. Hawk sighed and leaned his head wearily against the wall. *And I hide mine too well.*

Another crash echoed and then silence. Too much silence. Apprehension made Hawk step up to the closed door.

"Sara?"

Silence answered and a tiny niggle of panic pushed him forward.

"Dammit, Sara! Answer me or I'm coming in, clothes or no clothes."

Without further hesitation, he shoved his way into the tiny enclosure and was stopped in his tracks like a pole-axed steer. She was dressed . . . sort of dressed . . . in an oversize Dallas Cowboy T-shirt that barely covered *things*, and on her hands and knees swiping at the floor, commode, tub, cabinet. *It* was everywhere and it looked like . . .

"Don't say a word, mister," she said, a low, gritty warning in every syllable. "I made a mess. I'm cleaning it up. It probably wouldn't have even happened if you hadn't made me so angry, then I wouldn't have had this . . . this fit. I can't help it, anyway. I've tried. I just get a headache," she muttered. "I don't want to discuss this anymore. I just have slight lapses of control of my emotions. Roger knows it and now so do you. It's not my fault anyhow; it's in my genes."

Hawk raised one eyebrow sardonically, struggled briefly with a laugh that wanted out and then muttered, "You really are a little Wildcat aren't you. What is that stuff, anyway?'' He swiped his finger across the cloudy surface of the vanity and then carefully tested it for taste . . . and scent.

It definitely wasn't what he'd first suspected and breathed a quiet sigh of relief. He'd never seen or smelled any drug that reminded him of flowers. He allowed himself a tiny grin at the sight before him.

Sara glared up at Hawk from beneath the white cloud that hung thickly in the air like ash from Mount St. Helens. She mumbled and continued a rather futile clean-up effort.

"I'm sorry. I didn't hear what you said," Hawk drawled, laughter deepening his voice. He shoved his hands into his pockets and leaned nonchalantly against the doorframe. He was now grinning from ear to ear.

Sara had the most uncontrollable urge to fling what was left of the body powder in his face.

Hawk read her thoughts as if she'd flashed them computer style across her forehead.

"Don't even think it, lady."

Sara sighed as she crawled amidst the havoc she had created. Finally, she threw the damp rag down in disgust and slumped on the edge of the tub.

"I'll finish cleaning this up," she said as she looked about in dismay, "just as soon as it settles."

Dog padded down the length of the hallway and looked up at the stuff drifting about in the air. He sniffed curiously and then sneezed twice in succession. He looked first at the stranger sitting on the tub and then at his master.

"What's the matter, boy?" Hawk laughed, as he watched his pet's comical expression. All he got for an answer was a short, sharp bark from Dog before he turned and padded away toward the back of the house and quieter quarters. He wasn't used to such disruptions in his orderly routine.

"Your dog summed up this whole mess quite well," Sara said, venturing a slightly repentant smile and swiped limply at a small cloud of powder floating by her nose.

"You're one tough lady, aren't you, Sara?" Hawk thrust out a helping hand, as he lifted her from her seat on the edge of the tub. "I think it's time to get some food in you and then to bed. You need some quiet time after that bump on your head and I've some plans of my own to make."

Sara watched transfixed as the man Roger had promised Mackenzie Hawk to be emerged. His facial expression became fixed, harder. The green fire in his eyes banked until it was nothing but icy jade. Muscles tightened and flexed along the cut of his jaw and he grasped Sara's shoulders firmly as he spoke.

"I'll leave Dog here with you. You'll be safe and I won't be gone long." His words were short and concise, his voice hard. "I've more or less burned my bridges with the Company, but I still have a few friends that might be able to help me sort this out. Will you do what I say? Can I trust you to trust me?"

Sara sensed the clipped question held more meaning than just surface words. She suspected trust had been a rare commodity in this man's world. Yet for some reason, in spite of her earlier fury, trust in this big, angry man seemed to come easily to her. That, and this unexpected attraction she wasn't prepared to contemplate. Yet, there was something about Mackenzie Hawk that drew her. She saw him waiting tensely for her answer with a strange, guarded expression on his face.

"Trust? Yes, I trust you, Mackenzie Hawk. My brother

trusted you with his life and he said I could trust you with mine. I don't know if I like you yet, but I trust you."

Hawk nodded, accepting her statement as fair and then he gasped as she finished.

"How could I not trust you? You're my guardian angel, right?"

The look in her eyes took his breath away. She remembered more than he had realized about last night. Hawk looked down at her slender hand as she reached out and trustingly clasped it in the dark strength of his own. An ache started so deep inside him, he couldn't have found the source to save his life. If he wasn't careful, this woman could prove to be more dangerous to him than anything the Company had ever dreamed up. Hawk was afraid he couldn't walk away from Sara Beaudry as easily as he had walked away from the Company. But what scared him most was not wanting to. He didn't want to like Sara. She didn't belong in his world, and he damn sure didn't belong in hers.

THREE

Hawk made the drive south to Broken Bow, Oklahoma, in less than an hour in his 4×4 Blazer. He had debated with himself about driving in that direction to make his phone calls. That was the way Sara had come and there was the remote possibility that it would lead the wrong people back to her, but he took the chance. Hawk didn't like surprises. He figured the best way to eliminate them was to meet them head on. If anyone *was* following Sara from Texas into Oklahoma, chances were they would eventually come through Broken Bow. There weren't that many good roads leading to the Kiamichi. And there was always someone in town who noticed strangers. Broken Bow wasn't all that large, and the old men who sat on street benches in the summer had merely moved indoors to the little cafes and coffee shops. There, from the plate-glass windows, they still watched the world pass by over endless cups of coffee. If strangers came, they would know, and Hawk would find out.

Hawk stood in a phone booth near Main Street, reluctant

to make another call. There had only been two people Hawk remembered from his days with the Company who might be willing to help him. Unfortunately, his first phone call shortened the list to one. His first contact had been dead over a year. Hawk prayed as he dialed that this second call would not be futile. He hated the thought of having to contact the Company and Colonel Harris.

If the colonel was still in charge of Roger's division, he wouldn't tell Hawk anything. The man went by the book all the way. And since Hawk no longer belonged, he would be told nothing classified. In the Company, everything was classified.

But Hawk's luck held. A single phrase identified him and his contact willingly confirmed Sara's story in more detail than he cared to hear. Roger was indeed in hiding. Sara had interpreted the message correctly and had been wise in leaving Dallas. Word on the street was that someone big was involved. And to get to Roger, they wanted Sara. Someone powerful . . . deadly. *But,* Hawk thought as he hung up the phone, *weren't they all.*

Inconspicuously as possible, Hawk sought information as he gathered supplies for a long, enforced stay on the mountain. Buying extra quantities of foodstuffs was not unusual during the winter months because Oklahomans had to be constantly prepared for the possibilities of impassable roads and power failures. Unlike city dwellers, most rural people could not just drop in a store anytime they felt like it. There was an old saying among early day settlers, If you didn't like the weather in Oklahoma, just wait a bit, it would soon change. This prophecy was all too true and caused hardship unless one was prepared for any possibility.

With some extra clothing for Sara stuffed in among his

own purchases, the size differences were overlooked by the busy saleslady. That forestalled the obvious question of who the clothing was for. Everyone in the area knew Hawk's solitary state. It would be a choice bit of gossip to find out he had a visitor on the Kiamichi, especially a pretty female. And Sara's safety depended on secrecy.

Hawk's tight-lipped, steel-jawed expression gave away none of the anxiety he felt as he circled around the block, coming back down Main Street one last time and waving nonchalantly now and then at a familiar face. He was searching the traffic for out-of-state cars or strange faces. It was difficult to discern the difference between out-of-town visitors down for the Christmas holidays and strangers that had no place in Broken Bow, yet by the time he headed home, Hawk felt certain Sara had escaped Dallas unobserved.

He couldn't deny the conflicting emotions at war within him as he turned the last curve of the road home that snaked up the Kiamichi. It had been a long time since he had a reason for hurrying home; for someone to come home to. Pulling into the driveway, he forced back the pleasure that threatened. He didn't know why he was happy. There was a woman in his home who was probably going to drive him crazy before this episode came to an end. She was still somewhat of a mystery to Hawk. His moody reticence was at obvious odds with her fiery, volatile personality.

Mackenzie Hawk was a man of two worlds. He had walked a thin line dividing his Indian and white heritage all his life. Only Old Woman had understood his feelings of abandonment and loved him without question. But she was gone and Sara Beaudry had entered his life, breaching walls he'd built around himself. Hawk couldn't let her any further over them than she'd already climbed.

With resolve to ignore Sara fixed firmly in his mind, Hawk gathered his purchases from the Blazer and hurried toward the waiting warmth of home. He wasn't going to worry about anything more than solving this dilemma and then getting Sara Beaudry out of his life. Then, she opened the door to greet him.

The look on her face alerted Hawk to the fact that she hadn't passed the time in quiet repose as he'd instructed and somehow he wasn't the least bit surprised. He silently wondered if she'd ever once done as she was told.

"What's wrong," he asked as he entered with both arms full of sacks, kicking the door shut behind him as he gratefully inhaled the scents of home.

"Nothing," she muttered, refused to meet his eyes, and took a sack from him as she headed toward the kitchen.

Hawk watched Sara's retreating figure disappear along with his newfound resolve. Shifting his grocery sack to a better grip, he started to follow Sara into the kitchen. Movement by the sofa caught his eyes and Hawk glanced down at his pet who was at his usual place by the fireplace. Dog wagged his tail apologetically.

"She's got you buffaloed, too, hasn't she, boy?" Hawk mumbled. Where had all his determination to ignore her gone? He knew where. In the kitchen with the leggy redhead.

"I thought I told you to rest," Hawk grumbled, unloading groceries into the kitchen cabinets. He smelled something cooking.

Sara turned slowly, watching his face for some sign, some hint of what he'd found out while he'd been gone, but he was so solemn, and too still. She was suddenly very, very afraid. Her voice shook as she whispered.

"Has something happened? Is Roger okay? Please . . ."

and she leaned limply against the countertop, her legs suddenly too weak to hold her upright.

"Nothing happened," Hawk answered quickly, sorry his silence had been misinterpreted, "but you did read Roger's warning correctly. You *are* a prime factor in Roger's safety. Evidently, he's hidden himself well. The powers that be can't get to him. And if they can't find you either and force Roger's hand, you'll both be safe. The Company can deal with the situation if given enough time, so if that's what Roger needs, that's what we'll give him."

Relief made Sara's legs buckle. The roll of paper towels fell from her hands end over end, bouncing in awkward little wobbles as it came to rest at her feet. She swallowed hard . . . twice . . . trying to get out the words, but they wouldn't come. One tiny tear slid toward Sara's nose as she buried her face in her hands, trying to muffle the moan she felt crawling up her throat.

It was reflex that made Hawk catch her, but it was compulsion that made him gather her closely within the strength and safety of his arms. He was shocked by the way she fit within his arms. His chin rested just right on her crown of fiery curls. Breast to chest, arm in arm, she leaned into the narrow cradle of his hips as if she'd been carved to fit. *Damn but she feels good,* Hawk thought. He inhaled deeply, intoxicated by the feel of her and the flood of emotions sweeping through his senses as Sara threw her arms around him. But holding Sara was a feeling Hawk feared addictive and attempted to release her from his grasp.

Sara felt him withdrawing, yet she couldn't let go. She was holding on to the only solid substance in a world turned upside down. For the first time since the death of her parents, she felt unable to cope. Roger had been her rock, and now with his disappearance, Hawk was her only lifeline. Without his strength and confidence and the gentleness he tried to mask, she would be lost.

"Hawk . . . please," she pleaded, and buried herself deeper against the solid strength of his massive chest. He could respond no other way. He sighed and reluctantly gathered her closer.

"I know I'm an intrusion you don't want or need," she said, fighting back tears, "but you are all I have and I can't deal with this by myself. I'm over my head on this one. Will you bear with me?"

Tears pooled in her eyes and she bit a corner of her lip, worrying the softness as she tilted her head back and looked into the tension and concern drawn on Hawk's face. She waited anxiously for his answer.

You're not the only one in too deep, little Wildcat, Hawk thought. He reached down with the tip of his finger and stroked the velvety softness of her lip, traced the line to the corner she was biting, and gently pulled it away from her teeth.

"Sara," he said, his voice as gentle as his caress, "you've got me for as long as you need, and even if you were unexpected, you're not an intrusion. I've just been alone too long." *And lonely. I didn't realize how lonely,* Hawk thought.

He held himself in check, fighting the urge to taste the place on her lips where his finger had touched. If it tasted as wonderful as it felt . . .

Sara sighed, and once again lay her head against his chest, relishing the softness of the blue chambray shirt touching her cheek along with the smell of him, the feel of him. Musk and leather, faint traces of wood smoke, and Hawk. He was more man than she had ever known and Sara feared after this, no man would ever come close to his measure. *Roger, what have you gotten me into?*

Ill at ease and a little embarrassed, they stepped away from each other. Hawk bent down to retrieve the roll of paper towels and then turned away from Sara, refusing to look at her.

Muscles bunched and tightened across his shoulders, rippling down his back to the taut hip pockets of his Levis. He moved from table to cabinet and back again, putting away the remaining groceries while steadily ignoring Sara's presence.

Sara watched transfixed as he moved. Such grace and strength. A few moments ago those arms had held her, held her so closely she'd felt his heartbeat. Heard the slow steady beat break rhythm as she'd pressed against him. It would take very little imagination to recall the way Hawk had looked the first time she'd awakened to see him standing tall and bronzed, framed by a backdrop of flames from his fireplace, and wearing little more than he'd been born in. Mackenzie Hawk was all male, and probably more than Sara Beaudry had previously encountered.

She took a deep breath, refusing to be intimidated just because Hawk was ignoring her. Actually, it was a new experience for Sara to be ignored. Her fame usually prevented anonymity. However, she didn't think this was the time, or the man on which to experiment. She'd never admitted defeat in her life, and she wasn't about to start now. Besides, why should she care about what this infuriating man thought of her. She didn't even like him . . . at least she didn't think she did.

Hawk could feel her watching him from across the room and decided enough was enough. It was time to change the atmosphere.

"Something smells good," Hawk said, as he walked toward the back door of the kitchen to let Dog outside.

"Oh, the stew!" Sara cried, and dashed to the stove.

She fiddled with the lid on the stewpot and stirred the contents, ignoring Hawk's steady gaze. "I think it's about ready. Are you hungry?"

Sara was trying to inject a note of normality into the strained silence. She watched Hawk's dog disappear into the mouth of night and into the woods. "Isn't it too cold for him?" Sara asked. "It's starting to snow."

The first flakes were blowing against the window where they quickly melted and ran down the panes like scattered tears.

"He's used to it," Hawk answered. "Besides, he wouldn't stay in with me tonight. In fact, he'll probably be gone for quite a while." A long, mournful howl from outside punctuated his statement.

Sara's eyes widened and she shuddered, clasping her arms about herself as she realized for the first time the wildness of this part of the Kiamichi.

"Will they hurt him?" she asked, imagining a wolf pack fast on the big dog's trail.

But Hawk quickly stilled that fantasy and brought a blush to Sara's cheeks.

"No, Sara, he's not in danger. I think he's mated with one of the pack. It's not the first time and it won't be the last. The winter gets long and lonely on the mountain, and Dog hungers for companionship . . . as do we all."

Hawk grinned to himself. Sarah was embarrassed. She was such a contradiction and maybe that was what fascinated him. She wasn't afraid of anything, at least she didn't seem to be. She rode motorcycles like a biker, had temper tantrums befitting a true redhead, and then blushed like a schoolgirl at the mention of Dog taking a mate. Hawk decided to change the subject.

"Something's burning," he drawled.

"The stew!" she groaned and turned back to the stove to rescue their dinner.

They ate together in silence, finishing the meal as if they had done so many times before.

The last of the dishes had been put away and Sara and Hawk sat in comfortable silence by the fireplace, watching flames eat into a new log Hawk had just thrown onto the fire. Something Sara discovered during the time Hawk had been gone was bothering her and she looked deeply into the heart of the fire as she remembered what had caused her discontent.

"It's stuck," Sara muttered to herself as she struggled with a dresser drawer in the downstairs bedroom Hawk had assigned as hers for the time being. She gave it a hard yank and nearly fell as the drawer came open. She grunted in satisfaction and started to put her few bits of clothing and toiletries in it when she saw something tucked away in the corner of the drawer. There was an old, lavender sachet, some lace handkerchiefs, and a handful of cards and letters tied with a frayed, pink ribbon. This was the kind of stuff a woman would keep. Sara felt her heart skip a beat and then it felt like it fell clear to the pit of her stomach. A wife? . . . lover? . . . she didn't think she was going to like this turn of events.

Granted, she'd admitted to the inescapable fact that he was very, very sexy. So . . . lots of men were sexy. She'd certainly seen a few in her business. She'd even admit to an unwilling attraction to this man who'd been her brother's partner. It was the fantasy of having those magic eyes darken with passion, not anger, and the thought of being held in his arms, in his bed, all through the night, that made Sara shudder. Her hands shook as she reached down and picked up the packet of cards. She pulled slowly at the end of the pink tie and watched it fall loosely back into the drawer as she took the top card and, against all her better judgment, opened it. She knew she was trespassing. She just couldn't stop the urge compelling her to read the message inside.

It was an old Valentine covered with red hearts and flowers and a sweet, sentimental message . . . and it was signed, "All my love, Hawk."

If she didn't know better, the feeling that was swamping her senses could have been jealousy. But she didn't even like him. *Besides*, she scolded herself, *jealousy is reserved for lovers*.

Suddenly, she saw Hawk as a stranger would see him for the first time and she dropped limply to the bed, still clutching the stack of cards in her hands.

Tall, dark, and handsome didn't quite cover the strength and confidence he exuded without even trying. The stark mixture of the blending of his two worlds, had marked his face unforgettably. Memories of the emerald eyes and burnished copper glow of his body in the firelight came quickly to Sara's mind. She shivered in spite of herself at the memory, felt an unfamiliar heat in the pit of her stomach, and quickly branded it lust. Disgusted with her thoughts and her snooping, she shakily tied the cards back the way she'd found them and gently closed the drawer. Quietly, she left the room.

The rest of the afternoon she waited apprehensively for Hawk to return. And while she waited, she tried to come to terms with the new emotions pushing about inside her heart. For the first time in more years than she could count, Sara Beaudry felt attracted to a man. A man who'd made her fear him, yet she trusted him. A man who'd looked upon her with scorn, yet treated her with a gentleness she'd never experienced before. Roger trusted him, but could Sara trust herself enough to give this attraction a chance? He was so unlike anyone she'd ever known. But the thought had taken hold, and the seed of attraction was beginning to flower into more. And so she waited.

By the time she'd heard him coming up the road that led to the cabin, she'd worried herself into a frenzy of fear for her brother and for the situation that was swiftly getting out of her control; a growing need for Mackenzie Hawk to approve of her, to like her, and most of all, to trust her.

The wind popped around the sides of the cabin and whipped down the chimney in a short, fierce gust. It startled Sara's reverie and brought her thoughts back into focus.

It was not her way to skirt around any issue, so she took a deep breath and blurted out her question, although she greatly feared she was not going to like the answer. "A woman used to live here with you, didn't she, Hawk?"

Hawk was startled by the sudden break of silence, but not by Sara's question. He hadn't known her long, but was beginning to read her moods, and she'd been stewing about something ever since he'd come back from Broken Bow. Obviously, this was the something on her mind.

Lingering sadness tinged the green fire in his eyes and his face tightened, bracing himself against actually voicing his loss.

"Yes," he finally answered and looked once into Sara's eyes before turning back to the dance of flames in the fireplace.

Great! Sara thought, disgusted with herself for being nosey and for bringing such sadness to Hawk's eyes. *But that didn't tell me what I want . . . no, what I have to know.*

She debated with herself for several moments before she took another deep breath and plunged ahead with her cross-examination.

"Well?" she continued, picking nervously at the hem of her T-shirt. "Where is she now?"

"Dead."

The single word hung in the darkening room like a clap of thunder, echoing about the four walls and in Sara's heart.

"Oh, Hawk, I'm sorry," Sara blurted out, "I shouldn't have insisted you answer. It's none of my business." And she leaned across the length of the sofa, intent on offering a comforting touch when Hawk quickly stood, placing himself just out of her reach.

Sara sighed as she settled against the back of the sofa. She feared that was where Hawk would forever remain, just out of reach. And maybe he was the wiser of them for realizing the need to do so.

"It's time for bed, Sara. You've had quite a day."

Hawk's deep voice was gentle, apologizing in the only way possible for his retreat. He offered a helping hand, lifting her from her seat on the sofa.

"Yes, well," Sara mumbled, eyes downcast as she started down the hallway toward her bedroom.

Hawk watched her retreat and then shocked himself when he called out her name.

"Sara."

His voice behind her was compelling and she turned toward it, awaiting whatever would follow. Only his silhouette was visible as she stood at the end of the darkened hallway. She watched him hesitate, debating with himself before he sighed and jammed his hands into his pockets. Sara stood silently, waiting for him to continue.

She's not going to make it easy for me, Hawk thought, and grinned slightly to himself. *She doesn't make it easy for herself, why would I be any different?*

"The woman who used to live here with me . . ." Sara's silence was deafening and it hurt to say the words aloud, but he continued. "She wasn't my woman. She was my . . . she was the woman who raised me."

"Oh!"

What a wealth of understanding in such a small word. And what a relief. Sara's legs were shaking. She was surprised at herself, realizing how tensely she had awaited his answer.

"Hawk," her voice seemed suddenly very young and unsure.

"What now, little Wildcat? You know what curiosity did to its cousin, don't you?"

But Sara ignored his feeble attempt to change the subject.

"Don't you have any other family?"

"No."

The finality of his answer made her hesitate, but then she persisted.

"Why?"

The bitterness in his voice was unmistakable.

"Because I'm a bastard—a half-breed throw-away. A disposable commodity in one world and a burden for welfare in another. Old Woman took me . . . because no one else would."

"Hawk, I'm sorry," Sara whispered, and then realized she was talking to herself. He was gone. She blinked back tears as she listened to his footsteps on the stairwell. Hawk was headed toward his bedroom; his eyrie, high on the mountain.

Sara pulled the covers tightly under her chin, letting sleep creep softly into bed beside her. So beautiful, so strong, and so alone; Mackenzie Hawk, like his namesake, dwelt high on the mountain. And like the hawk, he circled life as the hawk circled the skies.

My beautiful, beautiful Hawk, Sara thought as she dreamed, her sanity fogged with confusion as she slept. But Hawk wasn't a bird, and he didn't belong to her. And maybe that was the reason for the tears that ran down her face while she slept.

And as she slept, safe and warm high on the Kiamichi, the search continued for the Texas Wildcat.

"Sir, I'm absolutely certain she left Dallas. I just don't know how or where. Well, if I may say so, sir," a sarcastic tone slipping into his voice, "if you'd let me contain the quarry when I first located it, you wouldn't have to be dissatisfied with me. I'm not too happy with the situation either. I do have a certain reputation to maintain."

A hard, implacable look came into his pale, blue eyes, making him suddenly appear very dangerous and very, very angry.

"Oh, I'll find her. I can guarantee that. But for now, you'll have to postpone your little game. Time is now on Beaudry's side and you have only yourself to blame."

The tracker disconnected. Suddenly, he was very weary of little men with too much money and too much power. But he'd been in this business too long to develop a conscience. The search would continue.

_____ FOUR _____

After five days and six inches of snow, Hawk was at his wit's end. Sara had to be one of the most exuberant individuals he had ever known. She had helped carry firewood from a workshed to the back porch three times, read everything of interest from his rather well-stocked bookshelves that bordered the fireplace, cleaned the house from top to bottom, and cooked everything she knew how to cook twice. Hawk considered himself fortunate that Sara was also sick and tired of the menu. She only knew four recipes by heart. Hawk knew he didn't want to eat anything that had hamburger in it for at least six months. Thank goodness he had run out of it in his freezer. They were now down to stuff Sara couldn't prepare. There was nothing left but venison, rabbit, quail, and squirrel.

Sara wrinkled her nose while sorting through the neatly wrapped packages in the small freezer chest. Hawk watched, mesmerized by the sight of her long legs and perfect backside squeezed into a pair of the tightest jeans he had ever seen a woman wear. The dark-green sweatshirt, one he had purchased for her during his trip to Broken Bow, fit fine. But he had misjudged the size of the pants. The tight fit didn't seem to bother Sara. However, it damn sure bothered him. He ached in places he couldn't locate, and some he could.

"Sara, quit fidgeting and come help me."

Hawk had been wrestling with some evergreen branches for a long time, trying to form them into a wreath. The wreath was recognizable, but not the wad of scarlet ribbon he was holding helplessly.

Sara's eye lit up when she spied the festive greenery. "A wreath! Are we going to decorate your house? Let me help."

"No, this is for something else." But her crestfallen expression made him add, "However, if you can make this mess into a passable bow and get it on this wreath, you can do whatever you want to the house when I get back."

"I don't want to decorate the house. I want to go with you. I'm sick of being indoors."

Her plea touched him, yet how could he explain where he was taking the wreath without hurting her feelings?

"Sara, I'd rather do this by myself. It's for Old Woman."

Sara turned away, blinking back tears that stung all the way down her throat as she attempted to hide the hurt. Hawk continually shut her away from anything personal. They had laughed and talked and shared companionable silences during the last few days, but each time Sara had ventured too close, Hawk clearly shut her out of his heart. He either didn't know how or didn't care to share himself. Yet, for a woman as generous and giving as Sara, it was unthinkable to be so alone.

"I understand. I didn't mean to intrude," she whispered. "I'm sorry, Hawk." She took the ribbon from his hands and walked out of the kitchen.

Her quiet voice and stiff posture while walking away revealed her pain, and Hawk sensed instinctively how she resented the distance he struggled to maintain between them.

Hawk ran a hand through the thick, shaggy hair that fell about his face and down onto his shoulders. He needed a haircut. He needed . . . he needed his head examined. *Sara won't intrude*, he thought. She was too sensitive for that. Hawk sighed and rose wearily from his seat. He knew why he kept shutting Sara out of his life. It was because he so very badly wanted her in it.

He found her sitting halfway up the staircase, her face hidden by the fall of her hair as she bent over the tangle of scarlet ribbon. Slowly and methodically, she picked the knots and twists from the ribbon and fashioned it into a cluster of red loops. With each tangle she released she muttered softly, and each loop added to the puffy bow set a fresh tear rolling down her face.

Damn, Hawk thought with a silent groan.

Each tear that rolled unchecked down her face was like a nail through his heart. The wreath hung limply from his fingers. He dropped it on the stair as he started toward Sara.

Suddenly aware of his presence, Sara swiped surreptitiously at her face, sniffed and then mumbled, "The bow is finished. If you'll hand me the wreath, I'll fasten it on for you."

"Sara," he whispered.

She studiously ignored his appeal and fiddled unnecessarily with the ribbon.

"Sara, look at me. Please."

His deep, husky voice beckoned, but it was the please

that did it. She turned her tear-stained face upward and saw her pain mirrored in his eyes.

At his quiet, "Come here, little Wildcat," she fell into his outstretched arms, sobbing softly against his chest.

"I'm scared all the time, Mackenzie Hawk. I'm afraid I'll never see Roger again. I'm afraid he'll die like my parents did and then I'll be all alone. And I can't tell just anybody about this mess. I can only tell you. But I don't think you hear me, Hawk. I don't think you listen."

Hawk was stunned at the depth of her fear and suffering, and remorse overwhelmed him.

"I'm sorry, Sara. I'm so, so sorry. I haven't even considered how frightening all this must be to you. It is so much a part of my old life, I simply fell into the game without considering all the players. Roger knew the score, I knew the rules, even the bad guys knew how to play. But you didn't did you, baby? You were thrown into it headfirst and I nearly let you drown."

His fingers combed gently through the mane of hair tumbling down her back. The curls wound and tangled, caught and held him in their clutches as surely as Sara Beaudry was holding his heart. Speaking in low, even tones, he soothed her hysteria as he rocked her gently in his arms.

The struggle to trust again was warring fiercely within him. Hawk wanted to believe Sara was real. He wanted to believe her actions were sincere. He wanted to . . . but something held him in check. He wouldn't, or couldn't, let go of the memory of another time and another woman . . . and her deceit.

Then, somewhere deep in the forest behind the cabin, a wolf howled. Its mournful call echoed in Mackenzie Hawk's soul. It would get dark early. *We can't linger,* he thought, *if Sara and I go down the mountain and back this afternoon.* As quickly as that his decision was made.

"Better bundle up, lady. You wanted fresh air, but you may get more than you bargained for."

His reward was the expression on her face.

"I won't be long. I'll fasten the bow on the wreath on the way." Her long legs took the stairs down, two at a time.

The walk down had been quick and silent. Sara knew this wasn't just any outing. She sensed how deeply Hawk had loved Old Woman. Sara had simply wanted to share his feelings. If anybody could understand emptiness, she could. *After all,* Sara remembered, *I buried both parents at the same time. Thank God I still have Roger.* Sara shuddered, blaming it on the cold, but she knew she would not feel safe until she saw her brother's smiling face again.

They had been walking through a stand of pines since leaving the cabin, and Hawk began to slow down as they approached a clearing. He had stayed away from the road for two reasons. One, the snow was not as thick under the trees, but hung on the branches instead, like wet clouds caught too low to the earth. And the other reason was, Hawk couldn't take any chances with Sara's welfare until he knew how secure her hiding place was. Soon, he feared, he would need to go back to Broken Bow, and when he did, his call would have to be to Colonel Harris. He would know for certain if Sara was still in danger.

"I think I'll rest here a bit, if you don't mind," Sara said, and handed Hawk the wreath with the bright ribbon fastened securely against the strong winter winds. She brushed the loose snow from a big rock that rested under the trees ringing the meadow, and gingerly sat down on the icy rest. Hawk took the wreath, silently acknowledging her thoughtful gesture.

Sara watched him leave the shelter of the trees and walk alone into the clearing. He walked into the pristine blanket that covered the meadow, his footsteps the only sign of life in the cold and silence of the Kiamichi. And then, he was on his knees, brushing away the snow from a stone that rose above the ground, erupting from the depths of the earth and forever pointing upward toward the light.

Sara looked away, suddenly afraid to see too deeply into Mackenzie Hawk. She might not be woman enough to watch.

"Are you ready?" Hawk asked, as he offered his hand and pulled Sara from her icy seat. "I think we better hurry. It takes longer to go up the mountain than come down, and it will be dark soon."

His deep voice broke the silence. Sara nodded her agreement as she brushed the snow from the seat of her pants. She looked back once. The wreath was the only bit of color as far as the eye could see. A tiny gift of love all green and red in a world frozen in starkest shades of grey and white.

Sara was puffing, definitely winded, as they neared the last stretch of trees before the cabin clearing. She mentally blamed it on her enforced inactivity.

"I'm going to be so chapped and out of shape when I get home, Morty will have a fit."

Sara grinned to herself, picturing the look on her manager's face if he could see her now. She was his bread and butter. For that matter, she was his cake, too. And her looks were definitely on the top of his list of priorities.

Hawk frowned as he listened to her chatter. He had

been so concerned with the present, he hadn't considered the future. Obviously, the future meant no Sara, and he didn't think he liked that thought at all. *And who the hell is Morty?*

Hawk turned, intending to hasten her progress, when a particularly heavily laden branch of snow decided to unload. It fell on Hawk so perfectly it might have been planned.

Sara took one look at the surprise on his face and the snow slipping in careless abandon down the collar of his sheepskin coat, and she dissolved in a fit of laughter that echoed throughout the forest. Each time she tried to stop and catch her breath, she would take another look at the expression on Hawk's face and collapse into hysterics.

"Think that's funny, do you?" he growled, and advanced toward her like a stiff-legged snow monster.

Too late, Sara realized his intent. She found herself flat on her back—up to her ears in the cold fluff.

"Hawk! No! Stop it, stop it. That's too cold," she pleaded, as he scrubbed her face with huge handfuls of the stuff. Sara caught her breath at the look of devilment in his eyes, read his intentions before he'd even moved, and shrieked, "Don't you dare, you fiend, not down my shirt."

Sara fought weakly against Hawk and the snow he was gleefully scrubbing in her face and down her neck, but it was no use. Finally, too weakened from laughter to move anymore, she gasped,

"Okay, you win. Do what you will," and flung her arms wide in mock abandon.

Suddenly, it was no longer a game. Heartbeats slowed in shock before speeding up into a pace almost too fast for breath. Sara felt Hawk's body grow tense . . . hard . . . hungry. She saw her own desire mirrored in the deepest part of his eyes. Jade glowed and flared until rationality became ashes. Each breath she took pushed the softness of her body up into the hardness of his hunger. A slow throb began deep in her stomach and spread throughout her being. Only Hawk could make it stop.

I knew it would feel like this, Hawk thought, as he felt himself falling into the heat of her golden eyes. He was swamped by a strange yet overwhelming need. Sara's eyes held a look he was afraid to trust. He'd imagined he'd seen that look in another woman's eyes a long time ago and his instincts had been wrong. Hawk didn't know if he could trust himself . . . and Sara . . . enough to take a second chance.

Sara's hair fell in wild abandon against the snow. Stray curls wrapped sensuously about his hands as he struggled with a need to bury himself so deep . . . Hawk shuddered with a fierce, overwhelming desire as he gently untangled the curls from his fingers and brushed a damp lock of hair away from her mouth, clearing the way to sweetness he could no longer resist.

"Hell," Hawk muttered. He leaned down, helpless with the need to taste and touch this beautiful, willful Wildcat. He denied himself no more and flicked a tiny bit of snow from the corner of her mouth with his tongue before tasting her lips completely. Then he was there, covering the chilled softness of her slightly parted lips with a hungry heat.

Sara's arms slid around his shoulders, pulling him closer and closer, trying to take him into her. Her fingers curled tightly into the shaggy, black pelt of his hair, wanting to belong to him . . . wanting to be with him . . . completely. Maybe then the ache would stop. Maybe then the fire would die. But it didn't work. The ache only grew and the fire flamed higher.

Sara opened her lips to plead with him, and Hawk took her breath into his mouth, swallowing her words as he completely claimed her lips. He took what she gave with a gentleness that brought tears to her eyes. Each time he released her lips, allowing a small rush of air to enter her lungs, he groaned, as if it pained him to part from her sweetness, if only for a moment. Then he would swoop, like a bird of prey, back to Sara and the lifegiving strength of her caress.

Sara reached blindly for Hawk. She searched with shaking hands beneath the heavy winter clothing for the brown satin skin, needing to touch him, yearning to feel his body warm with life and a promise of passion. She felt his mouth at her temple and then in her hair, constantly searching and tasting; felt a sharp nip at the base of her throat where life pulsed wildly through delicate, blue veins and she groaned.

"Hawk, please," she begged through swollen lips, but Hawk needed no further urging.

He was past all rational thought and was acting on instinct. He needed to touch her fully, skin to skin, heartbeat to heartbeat. He wanted her to feel the hunger and wildness that had claimed his sanity.

Her coat was spread open against the snow, yet Sara felt no chill. She was on fire so deeply within, only Hawk could save her. Only Hawk could put out the fire . . . if it didn't consume her first.

Hawk was straining against her body, pressing her deeper and deeper into the snow, straining against the restrictions of their clothing, blindly trying to ease the pressure building inside him. He found the tail of her sweatshirt, slid his hands under the fabric, searching for the ivory perfection he knew was there and touched the warm, satin skin. He shuddered, remembering how she'd looked as he held her naked in the tub of warm water the night they met, and it made him want her more. He searched gently, desperate to feel Sara, to taste, to take, and he shook with hunger and need as his hands caressed and filled themselves on her breasts. Her heartbeat was wild beneath his fingers, yet it wasn't enough. He leaned down, craving a taste of the swollen nub pushing against his hand.

But reality intruded, and Hawk's well-trained instinct for survival pulled his subconscious back from the brink of insanity. Hawk stilled. His breathing slowed, and he listened.

Shock brought Sara back to reality much quicker than any words could have. The look on his face scared her to death until she realized she wasn't the cause.

Hawk yanked her roughly to her feet with disregard for the state of her undress and shoved her toward the cabin, fear taking command of his behavior.

"Run, Sara. Run as fast as you can for the cabin," he ordered, his words low and ominous. "Go to my bedroom . . . in the closet . . . guns are loaded. Hide until I come for you," he said, giving her shoulders a fierce, quick shake. "Remember, I'll come for you, only me. Don't answer to anyone else."

And she obeyed without question, for even she could now hear the familiar chop, chop, chop of a helicopter as it neared the cabin. Her heart beat in rhythm with fear as she obeyed Hawk's command. She ran up the back porch and through the kitchen. Her feet barely touched the staircase in the living room as she headed for Hawk's room.

She crawled on her hands and knees, below the clothes hanging neatly, beside the rows of boots matched and polished, and found the guns. Slowing her breath till it became a mere whisper, she squatted down against the darkest corner inside the closet, drew her knees up under her chin, and prayed for Hawk's safety . . . and for hers.

It came out of the setting sun, low and fast, just skimming the treetops like a dragonfly in summer that dances dangerously just above the level of the water. The sound of the rotor was in his ears and his heart beat in rhythm as the blade whirled, holding the chopper at rooftop level. It quickly circled the open area around the cabin, fanning the snow into a tiny blizzard of ice shards before dropping straight down.

Hawk shielded his face from the flying ice and snow as best he could, but it flew so wildly through the air, it pelted his face like icy needles against skin. Although the chopper had caused a tumultuous snowstorm of confusion, Hawk was not confused. His thoughts were cold and calculated as he set his quickly-formed plan into action. He had to be careful. Sara's life and his depended on it.

As two heavily-clad, hooded figures emerged from the chopper, Hawk took advantage of the frenzy of ice and snow to make his move.

The men crouched, using the hoods of their parkas to shield themselves from the maelstrom the helicopter had fanned into being. When the chop, chop, chop of the helicopter had disappeared over the treetops, the men stood erect, orienting themselves while wiping away the ice crystals from their eyes and faces. Peering through the settling snow, they saw the cabin standing dark and blurred in the fast-fading light of day, and began walking toward it.

They had a heartbeat's warning of the movement behind before the larger of the two men lay unconscious, facedown in the snow. The other had taken that fraction of a second's warning to fend off a similar blow. Instead, he and his attacker rolled wildly about in the snow-covered yard, stirring up a small blizzard of their own. The dusky silence was broken only by an occasional grunt of pain or a deep, harsh gasp for breath as the struggle continued. Finally, the man had gained enough space and time from his attacker to choke out a cry.

"Hawk, for God's sake man, stop! Stop I say! It's Harris, Colonel Harris. I've come to talk."

He prayed his words had penetrated the cold fury of his attacker or he was in serious trouble. He'd been behind a desk too long to handle a man like Mackenzie Hawk, and his companion was certainly in no shape to help him.

Harris crouched on hands and knees in the lowering temperature of late evening. His companion had warned him this was the wrong approach to take, but time was at a premium and lives were at stake, including his . . . if he couldn't call Hawk off.

Damn! Hawk thought as he straightened, mentally discarding the next set of blows he'd been planning to deliver. He walked slowly through the snow, his footsteps dragging from exertion and an overdose of adrenalin. Barely glancing at the colonel, he went instead to the man lying facedown in the snow. As Hawk rolled him over onto his back, the man's eyelids fluttered and he reached a shaky hand to his forehead.

"What hit me?" he mumbled, weakly testing his jaw to see if it would open, or fall off his face like it wanted to do.

"I did, you sonofabitch. What kind of stunt do you call this?"

Hawk was so furious he could barely talk. He still wanted to throttle something, or someone.

"Well, Colonel Harris, I told you this wasn't wise," Roger Beaudry said. He groaned weakly while rolling over onto his feet. "After all, I did send Sara to him for protection and giving him no warning . . . we were asking for . . ."

Hawk started at the mention of Sara's name and spared neither of the men a further glance as he bolted toward the cabin with renewed strength.

She must be petrified, he thought, dashing through the living room and up the stairs, his boots leaving tracks of snow that quickly melted into puddles from the warmth of the cabin.

Crouched in the closet, the helicopter sounded like an apocalypse as it hovered and circled the cabin. But now it was gone and all Sara knew was silence, loudly mocking her fear while she hid in the depths of clothes and shoes like a corpse in a cedar-lined crypt.

A door banged downstairs and heavy footsteps came rushing up the staircase as sweat ran down between her breasts and the middle of her back. Her heartbeat was so loud, her fear so thick, she was afraid she could be detected behind the heavy closet door.

"Sara!"

The shout came loud and clear, even into the depths she was hidden. It was the most beautiful sound in the world. The closet door flew open. Sara dropped the gun she was clutching and slid upright against the closet wall, squinting in the unaccustomed light. She pushed aside hangars of clothing, saw Hawk standing before her, and began to shake. She tried to speak, but words wouldn't come. She tried to walk, but her legs threatened to give way.

He looked wild and partially frozen, like an ancient warrior beginning to thaw after eons of suspended animation. Snow was melting from his heavy coat and pants and ran in rivulets onto the shiny hardwood flooring. His hair was wet and plastered against his head like an ebony helmet and his eyes glowed like frozen jade. He was magnificent . . . and she'd never been so happy to see anyone in her whole life.

"It's okay, Sara. It's okay; come here, baby," Hawk said as he pulled her shaking body into his grasp and held her tightly.

Roger and Colonel Harris came up the stairs in time to see Sara stagger from her hiding place and Roger's heart twisted painfully when his sister fell limply into the big man's grasp.

Damn this job! I've just put Sara through hell and this latest stunt the colonel pulled didn't help one bit. Then his eyes widened. A glimpse of Hawk's face as he cradled Sara into his chest shocked him. *Boy, oh boy! I've really done it this time*, Roger thought. *Damned if Hawk isn't in love with her . . . or so very nearly so it makes little difference*. Roger's thoughts whirled with the endless problems this latest development could produce.

Sara spoke, her voice weak and muffled from deep within Hawk's arms. She tried in vain to regain her equilibrium but it was no use, so she clung helplessly to Hawk's strength.

"What was it, Hawk?" Her voice shook as she continued. "Have they found me?"

Hawk's answer was as gentle as his demeanor as he turned Sara's face toward him, assuring her of her safety. "No. It's not the bad guys, baby. We've just got a little company." He turned her in his arms to see the rather shamefaced pair who stood dripping in the doorway.

"Roger! Oh, my God, Roger! Are you okay? Did they hurt you?" Sara tore herself from Hawk's arms and flung herself in Roger Beaudry's direction. "Is it over now, Roger? Is it safe for me to go home?"

Each shrill cry Sara uttered as she flew toward her brother's smiling face was a fresh tear in Hawk's very soul.

This is a damn nightmare, Hawk thought, and closed his eyes, trying to block out the sight of Sara as she fell from his grasp into someone else's arms. *Not again,* he groaned.

Cold rage wiped all rational explanation from his mind. All he could see was another woman, in another time, running toward . . .

He shuddered, wiped a shaky hand across his eyes and blinked, focusing in on the present.

"Shall we continue this fiasco in a somewhat drier part of the house?" Hawk asked sarcastically, hiding his pain behind a cold, emotionless demeanor. He pushed past the stunned trio to lead them downstairs.

Sara was bewildered by the change in his behavior; at a loss to understand it. Her earlier words, uttered in relief at the sight of her brother, were already forgotten as she tried to puzzle out this latest development in Hawk's attitude.

Amenities were uttered stiffly as Hawk hung wet clothing by a kitchen heater to dry. He ushered Sara and the men to warm seats by the fireplace. Working in silence, he added wood to the brightly burning fire, offered huge fluffy towels to dry what they could of their hair and clothing, and then disappeared into the kitchen.

Sara watched her brother and the man they called Colonel look at each other in unspoken agreement before Roger shrugged and turned to face his sister's questioning stare.

Cups and saucers clinked sharply against one another, signaling the forthcoming of some hot refreshment from the kitchen. Sara rose from her seat, her hands on her hips, and confronted the suspicious acting pair of men before her.

"Well, let's have it. Don't play around with me either." Sara searched Roger's face, only inches away as she angrily continued. "What's the big secret? I've been thrown in the middle of something I don't understand and I want some answers."

Roger took a deep breath, wiped sweaty palms on his pants legs, and looked to the Colonel for guidance. All he got for his trouble was a grimace and a shrug. *Damn!* Roger thought, *I've seen the Colonel tackle Company operations fraught with danger, face certain death from unfriendly fire, and sweet talk the most devious of foreign dictators, but he folded like a used napkin in the face of one Texas redhead.*

"There's no easy way to say this, Sara," Roger said. "You don't need details, most of them are classified, anyway."

"You're dithering, Roger Beaudry. Get to the point. Is this mess over or not? I can't hide forever. I have a rather promising career going slowly to pot at this time, thanks to you. What is all of this about anyway?"

The Colonel interrupted, and with his usual lack of aplomb, alienated his audience.

"Look, Miss Beaudry, we've got the situation under control. At least we do for the moment. Your brother was pulled in at fourteen-thirty hours yesterday afternoon. His safety was of paramount importance to the Company due to vital information he possessed about a certain . . . individual. Now that he's safe, and . . . if things go according to plan, we should have the bad guys, as you call them, out of circulation within a matter of days, and you back in circulation soon after. How does that sound?" His pompous expression slid down his face like hot butter at Sara's disgusted reply.

"It sounds like an awful big crock of . . ."

"Sara!" Roger's shocked remonstration did nothing to deter her from continuing.

"Let me get this straight, Colonel. You saved my brother because you needed information he possessed and if I'll roll over and play dead for a few more days, figuratively speaking, of course, you'll use that information, clean up this mess, and send me merrily on my way."

"Well, that's rather harshly put, Miss Beaudry."

"It's a harsh situation, Colonel Harris," Sara drawled.

The trio sat in stiff silence, none willing to give an inch as Hawk entered the room with a tray of steaming cups and set it down on the coffee table with a thud. Hot liquid sloshed carelessly into the saucers underneath the cups, filling the room with the scent of hot noodles and chicken.

"Soup's on," Hawk muttered, and stepped away from the tray he'd rudely served to lean against the rock wall of the fireplace. Standing defiantly, Hawk jammed his fists in his pockets, stretching the denim fabric tautly across his muscular thighs. He stood with legs apart, bracing himself for a mortal blow. The expression on his face tore at Sara's heart. Hawk looked so lonely . . . and hurt. *What has happened?* Sara worried. *What have I done to cause this defensive attitude?*

Hawk was back in that familiar shell Sara had fought so valiantly to crack, and this time, he seemed too far in to pull back.

"What's wrong, Hawk?" she asked, her undertone low and questioning. All she received for her concern was a slight sneer before he turned to face his guests.

"When are you leaving?" Hawk blurted out.

The rude question took them all by surprise. Sara

inhaled sharply. She thought she was beginning to understand his behavior. He didn't want her to go! And she'd rushed from his arms to her brother's arms with the request on her lips and little regard for his feelings. She'd practically begged to go back. Hawk must think her cold and shallow. *After all,* Sara thought, *if the helicopter hadn't arrived when it had, Hawk and I would have made love in the snow, without a thought for tomorrow.*

Roger winced, reading the hurt in his old friend's voice as he answered. "In the morning early . . . if you'll permit us to stay tonight." He was hurting for Hawk, and hurting for Sara, but helpless at this time to change the situation.

"In the morning," Hawk muttered, shocked and shaken at the emotions flooding through his mind and had to turn away to hide the devastation he felt at Roger's words. He hunched his shoulders, bracing himself once more against the pain of loss.

Sara felt his pain as if it were her own.

"Hawk, please . . . can we talk?" she pleaded, but was interrupted by the Colonel's voice booming into the conversation.

"I believe you two misunderstand the situation we are dealing with at this time."

Both Sara and Hawk turned to face him, puzzled at the hurried explanation as he continued.

"Agent Beaudry and I are leaving in the morning. However, Miss Beaudry, we require you to remain here, with Hawk's permission, of course, for the time being."

The sheer relief Hawk felt at the Colonel's words was overshadowed by a dawning comprehension of the situation, and he didn't like what he was thinking. He didn't like it one bit.

"But why do I stay if Roger's okay?" Sara asked.

The Colonel's answer never left his lips as Hawk's angry voice filled the room.

"That's just it, isn't it, Beaudry," Hawk accused. "Everything is not okay. But the question then arises, if everything's not okay, why come swooping down in a helicopter over these Oklahoma hills where everyone still runs out to look as one flies over, if you are trying to stay unobserved." Hawk pointed a finger in Roger's face. "You wanted to be seen."

Roger couldn't face the fear and confusion on Sara's face. Her eyes were wide and frightened as she listened to the anger in Hawk's voice. It made Roger want to throttle Harris, but he didn't have a choice in the matter. Roger took his orders from a higher authority, and it sat in silence beside him while Hawk's derision and anger ate into his conscience.

Sara looked about in confusion, trying to make some sense of all these unfinished sentences and half threats when Hawk's final accusation made her sink limply onto the arm of the sofa.

"You're going to use her for bait, aren't you?"

When no one would deny the accusation, Hawk flew into a rage as Roger sat guiltily by his own silence.

"Damn it all to . . ." Hawk ran his hand roughly through his hair in frustration, "She's a civilian, Colonel. You can't drag her into an operation like this. The phone call I made earlier this week indicated heavy action. She's not equipped for this, mentally or physically. She's already had enough."

"It's Levette," Roger said quietly.

"Damn it, Beaudry," the Colonel snarled, "that's classified."

Hawk stilled and his countenance grew hard and ugly.

Sara shivered, suddenly afraid, and this time she was afraid of Hawk.

"He doesn't know *you* have her, Hawk," Roger said, ignoring his commanding officer's angry look. "But he does know she's in hiding. That's one point in our favor. He doesn't know I've been pulled in either. That's another plus. And the only way Sara's ever going to be safe again is if he's caught. I don't know how he found out about her. I never even told you I had a sister and this is why," Roger said, gesturing toward Sara, "I didn't ever want her to have to go through this on my account."

Roger's head slumped forward and he buried his head in his hands, ashamed to meet his sister's face. But he had under-estimated Sara Beaudry. She was at his feet in an instant. With tears in her eyes and voice, she pulled his head onto her shoulder and held him close.

"It's okay, honey," Sara whispered. "I didn't understand. None of us asked for this, but we've got it to face. I suppose the best thing to do is proceed with your plan. There doesn't seem to be any alternative. At least we can if Hawk will let me stay?" She turned toward him, blinking back tears as defiantly as she asked the question.

Hawk nodded his acceptance. "I don't like using her," he said, "but Levette won't touch her. You can count on that."

Sara shivered at the fury in his voice.

FIVE

"Sara, are you awake?"

Roger bent over Sara as she slept and pulled the pillow away from her face. Repeating the old, familiar habit made him smile. As a small child, Sara had always covered her head completely while sleeping, and Roger had been convinced she would suffocate.

"I am now," she mumbled. "What do you want?"

Roger also remembered a little late that Sara didn't wake up friendly. But there were some things between them that needed to be said and no time to waste.

"To talk. I need to explain."

Sara's voice, still husky from a deep sleep, cut him short.

"No, Roger . . . all this mess . . . it's okay, really. I don't mean it's okay that I'm involved. I mean I understand that it's not your fault."

Roger shuddered as he clumsily patted his sister's shoulder and whispered softly into the darkness of Sara's room.

"Sara, honey, you don't know how frightened I was

when I discovered Levette knew about you. He's merci-
less. In all the years I've been with the Company, he's
the most heartless bastard I've ever investigated.''

"Sit!'' Sara ordered, scooting over underneath her bedcovers and patting the bedside. Roger accepted her invitation gratefully and sat down, leaning his back against the
headboard of Sara's bed. It had been a long day.

"Does the Colonel know you're here?'' Sara questioned.

"No, but I don't much care one way or another. There
are some things I think you need to know and I'm not
going to be negligent with your safety because something's
classified. You mean more to me than any job, Sara. You
know that, don't you?''

No words were necessary. Sara's hug sufficed.

Way into the early hours of the morning they talked.
Hushed whispers behind closed doors reassured Sara as
nothing else could of the sincerity of Roger's remorse and
the severity of danger threatening. Her disappearance had
been explained and her job had been secured. A story that
wasn't as farfetched as she would have chosen was given
as the reason for her sudden disappearance. A family
emergency was as close to the truth as it came, and it had
calmed the uproar in Dallas when Sara disappeared. Sara
hadn't worried as much about her career as she had her
brother's safety. Sometimes she could almost welcome the
decision be made for her to discontinue modeling. She'd
raced with the rats entirely too long.

Sara's eyes burned and her throat was raw. She and
Roger had talked too long and slept too little. But Roger
was safe.

Everything seemed to be better, everything . . . except
her relationship with Mackenzie Hawk. They were back
to square one. With the arrival of Roger and the Colonel,
he'd simply shut her back out of his life. Hawk didn't

play by rules. Sara suspected if there were any rules in his life, he made them to suit himself.

Roger eased himself from Sara's bed, hoping to leave without disturbing her uneasy slumber. But he was sadly mistaken, believing he had relieved all of Sara's concerns. There was still one question Sara needed answered.

"Roger, why is Hawk so bitter about this . . . Levette? He scared me tonight when he repeated the man's name. I've never felt or seen so much hate."

Roger paused at the door. His answer was slow in coming as he walked back to Sara's bedside.

"Levette is evil. He deals in drugs, prostitution, firearms, anything that makes money, big money. He doesn't let anyone get in his way, and if they do, he eliminates them . . . and laughs."

"But that doesn't explain the personal vendetta I sensed, or is that classified, too?" Her need to know everything about Hawk was overwhelming.

"Most of it. But maybe you *should* know this much. Hawk's last assignment while still working for the Company was undercover in one of Levette's strongholds around the Florida Keys. Unfortunately, the Colonel, in his infinite wisdom, decided not to inform Hawk that he was being used to uncover a leak in our security. The Colonel decided to plant a couple of our people inside Levette's organization. Hawk was one of the plants. And a woman named Marla Ranko, the other Company infiltrator, was to be Hawk's liaison . . . she became his partner . . . and more."

Sara started. The mere thought of another woman lying in Mackenzie Hawk's arms made her want to throw things. She felt like screaming and crying all at the same time. Instead, she did neither. She sat quietly, urging her brother on by her silence.

"Well," Roger continued, "to make a long story short, Marla was the leak. Colonel Harris and his superiors had suspected it for months. They just didn't see the need to pass along their information or suspicions until they could prove them." Then Roger's voice grew quiet and grim. "But they should have told Hawk. It nearly destroyed him."

Roger paused, allowing his thoughts to gather and calm as he scooted to a more comfortable position against Sara's headboard. He pulled Sara comfortingly onto his wide, burly chest and buried her nose into the thick pile of his soft sweater as he continued. "That's where it got all screwed up."

Sara was silent, horrified by the situation Hawk had been unwittingly thrown into, and was beginning to understand his resentment toward the Company and its idea of loyalties. She listened, eyes widened in horror, hurting for what Hawk must have gone through as his life unwound before him.

Roger understood her distress, yet for her sake he continued, wanting her to understand the full scope of the situation.

"The Colonel hadn't expected an attraction to develop between Marla and Hawk or he might have reconsidered."

Roger felt Sara tense, but it was better she knew now before she got hurt. Roger loved Hawk like a brother. He'd sent his sister to him for protection. He'd trusted him with his life many times and knew Sara was as safe with Hawk as she would have been with him. But Mackenzie Hawk was a hard, embittered man. Roger took a deep breath and then continued.

"It was the night of the arrest, only nothing was going as planned. Hawk was unaware of anything at this point and was on his way to Marla's room to collect her and

escort her to dinner. Levette insisted on such formalities,"
Roger explained. "Unfortunately for Hawk, she wasn't
alone, and after her initial shock at being discovered in
Levette's arms, Marla refused to leave Levette. Hawk was
furious. I don't know all the details, only what Hawk put
in his report. Thanks to Marla Ranko, Hawk was caught
hands down. He was so taken aback by his discovery, he
didn't realize Company men had invaded Levette's strong-
hold until he heard the commotion on the stairwell outside
Marla's room. He pulled himself together, identified himself as an agent of the government, and started to arrest
Levette. Marla stepped between the two men just as the
door burst open. Levette took advantage of the confusion
to grab a handgun from Marla's bedside table. I still don't
know whether or not it was an accident, but in all the
turmoil, Marla took a bullet meant for Hawk. To top the
whole fiasco off royally, Levette got away. We still don't
know how."

"Ah . . . dear Lord," Sara whispered. "No wonder
Hawk blames Harris . . . and all women in general."

Tears rolled freely down her face as she looked at her
brother in stunned disbelief.

"Harris had superiors, too, Sara. It wasn't all his fault.
He's not bad or necessarily wrong. He's just by the book
all the way."

Roger worried he'd said too much to Sara, and then
worried he hadn't said enough. "Sara, honey, I'm sorry.
But you need to understand Levette. That's why I told
you. Also, you need to understand Mackenzie Hawk.
Don't judge him too harshly. Life already has."

When Sara awoke several hours later, the sun was shining, the snow beginning to melt, and robins and sparrows,
along with a multitude of other tiny snowbirds, were quar-
reling noisily in the treetops for the forage that appeared

as the snow disappeared. Roger and his commander were gone. Once again she found herself alone with Mackenzie Hawk, high on the Kiamichi.

"I have some news for you, sir. No . . . I don't know for certain where, but I believe a general vicinity has been narrowed down. We believe she is in the mountains of eastern Oklahoma. I have my sources, that's how I know," the tracker snapped. "A beautiful woman is a hard woman to hide, especially one so well-known. Give me a week, maybe . . ."

He was cut short and a frown deepened the weathered look about his pale-blue eyes. "I realize you have a schedule to keep, so do I. You'll be hearing from me soon."

He hung up the phone, paid for his gas, bought himself a package of Tootsie Rolls, and headed toward Oklahoma. He didn't have any noticeable vices, any distinguishing facial features or scars, and drove an older model car like most of the highway travelers. One never saw him coming until it was too late, and when he was gone, there was never anyone left to identify him.

He stood to collect a small fortune on delivery of the woman, and as far as he was concerned, absolutely nothing or no one stood in his way. It was what he did for a living.

The tracker sighed in satisfaction as the thick, coffee-flavored chocolate of the Tootsie Roll slowly dissolved into the sticky, chewy, texture he craved. A small thing, this penchant for an old childhood treat, and the tracker drove on into Oklahoma, Land of the Red Man.

"Where is everybody?" Sara called, as she wandered through the cabin.

The floors and furniture gleamed and a fresh, lemony

odor wafted through the air. Fresh cedar boughs had been cut and lay in decorative abandon on the mantle over the fireplace. Their distinctive fragrance blended with lemon oil and a lingering coffee smell assured Sara that Hawk was not far away. After yesterday's panic, Sara knew Hawk would not leave her alone again.

The rooms looked like Hawk was doing his best to welcome the Christmas holidays. A tiny handcarved creche complete with Joseph, Mary, the Christ Child, and an assortment of miniature animals rested in honor on a table against the living room wall. Sara stroked the neck of a tiny burro, so detailed it looked like it could bray any moment.

Sara marveled at the impeccable room and holiday decorations. They were quite a feat for a bachelor such as Hawk. Smiling thoughtfully, she wandered into the kitchen. The sound of an axe biting into wood at measured intervals told Sara which direction to look for her misplaced guardian angel.

Sara grabbed a jacket hanging from a peg beside the back door, shrugged into the gargantuan folds, and stepped outdoors into the sharp bite of early morning air. The fresh, clean scent of evergreen and newly-cut wood assailed her nostrils.

Hawk's coat lay carelessly across a stack of unsplit logs; his red plaid work shirt the only splash of color in the winter landscape. He was chopping and stacking the seasoned logs into firewood length with ease. Fascinated, she watched the play of his muscles as they gathered in strain, pulling the fabric of his shirt and Levis taut across his back and down his hips and thighs. *So big . . . so strong. Was it only yesterday we went to Old Woman's grave?* Sara wondered.

It seemed a lifetime had passed since Sara had lain

beneath Mackenzie Hawk, oblivious to anything except the intense passion that flared between them. At the thought, heat and instant longing welled, weakening her knees so that she grabbed hold of the porch railing for support. All she had to do to call back that feeling was close her eyes and the wild, out-of-control sensation claimed her so intensely, Sara imagined she could still feel the hard length of Hawk pressing against every aching portion of her body. She had never in her life wanted a man as she had wanted Mackenzie Hawk. And he had reciprocated. Sara knew that much. She had felt his need, desperate and wild as her own heartbeat. She took a deep, calming breath and forced her thoughts back to sanity. She couldn't face Hawk like this. He would know instantly what she had been thinking.

Dog's tail thumped a laconic welcome as Sara stepped off the porch onto the thawing earth. Melting snow lay in mirrored puddles between the house and woodpile as Sara picked her way carefully toward Hawk.

"Need any help?" she asked. Her thoughtfulness was rewarded with silence.

Okay, she thought, watching the axe fall with increased tempo, *maybe he just didn't hear me.*

"Hawk," she said a bit louder, "do you want this wood stacked here or carried to the cabin?"

This time he acknowledged her presence with a long, slow look that masked his thoughts quite thoroughly and irritated Sara no end.

"If a staring match is what you want," she muttered, and thrust her chin out in mutinous defiance.

Hawk raised an eyebrow, mocking her show of spirit, as his silence had mocked her offer of help. But Sara held her ground. Finally, he drawled, "You real sure you want to carry this dirty, heavy wood? I didn't think high-class . . . models . . . did manual labor. Might break a nail."

His taunt hurt. They were back . . . no, worse than they had been when they first met. But Sara was not a redhead for nothing. She had bulldog determination to match.

"They'll grow. Besides, haven't you heard of sculptured nails?" she asked.

"Yeah . . . aren't they fake, like the rest of your world?"

Sara spun away, unwilling for Hawk to see how his words struck home and blinked away angry tears. She answered him, spitting her words out through tightly clenched teeth.

"My world, as you call it, may be fake, but I'm not. I'm real, Hawk, and whether you like it or not, I'm here."

Hawk was ashamed of the way he kept hurting Sara, but his self-preservation depended on it. Sara Beaudry was a luxury he couldn't afford and until this mess with Levette was settled, a danger to herself as well as to him.

Sara balanced a couple of sticks of firewood precariously and started toward the stack by the porch steps. Hawk grabbed her by the arm and spun her sharply about, throwing the heavy wood aside in anger as he shouted.

"I don't want your help, Sara. I don't want anything from you. I thought I had made myself perfectly clear."

"You are hurting me, Hawk," Sara gasped, and tried vainly to wrench her arm free from his grip.

"No! Levette will hurt you. I'm just warning you. Go inside!" The angry words seemed more a promise than a threat.

Sara shivered, for the first time in her life suddenly aware of her mortality.

"Hawk, please," she begged, her voice losing its former bravado, "Why are you being so cruel? Yesterday in the snow you were . . ."

"Yesterday was a mistake."

"How can it be a mistake when two people care for each other?" Sara asked. His answer stunned her with its brutality.

"Care? That wasn't care. That was lust, lady. And lust is a passing fancy, just like you. When all this is over, you'll pass from my life like you were never here. I have no intention of living my life with two female ghosts in this cabin. One is enough."

Then, even Hawk felt the harshness of his sentence by the stricken look Sara wore. His next command was uttered softly and wearily.

"Go inside, Sara Beaudry. It's not safe out here in the open. Until Levette is captured, you'll never be safe."

Hawk watched Sara walk slowly into the cabin, her steps dragging. Somewhere inside him there began a pain so fierce, Hawk feared he was beginning to die. Twice he started to call Sara back, beg her forgiveness for the unspeakable way he had treated her. Beg her for . . . no, take all she had to offer, here and now. But each time, good sense held him back. She didn't belong here and she damn sure didn't belong to him. Until Levette was captured, Hawk couldn't afford to let anything distract him from Sara Beaudry's safety. It had to come first.

Hawk was at his wit's end . . . again. He'd spent as much of the day as possible outside the cabin until the quickly dropping temperature drove him inside. The forecasted storm was fast approaching. The weather forecasts on the radio had been continually interrupting programming all day long with bulletins warning of the impending snowfall.

Damn! Hawk thought. *This is all I need; to be snowed in with her at this point in our lives is suicide . . . or murder . . . whichever comes first,* he thought wryly.

Sara was in her room. She disappeared as soon as she heard Hawk come inside.

Hawk heard the door's decisive slam as soon as he entered the cabin and sighed. It was obvious from the lack of dishes in the sink that she hadn't eaten all day. He felt guilty, but not quite certain how to rectify the situation. He couldn't have her starve herself. She was already too thin for her own good. After the way he'd treated her, he supposed he should be grateful he wasn't the entreé. The problem was going to be how to get Sara to eat food without Hawk wearing it instead.

He went upstairs to his room, quickly stripped out of his grimy workclothes, and wearily stepped under the pelting jets of the shower head. He let the hot, steamy water wash away the tension he was feeling along with the day's dirt. He braced himself against the shower walls with arms outstretched, easing the muscles in his back and arms that were tight and aching from the hard workout with the axe and relentless resistance of seasoned wood.

Hawk watched the water run down his body and escape through the tiny metal holes in the bottom of the drain, and was reminded of the water in Sara's bath the first night they met; how it had lapped and caressed at her ivory curves. His body reacted against his will. He yearned to feel her again as he had yesterday in the snow. Hawk closed his eyes and groaned, remembering the sensations. Her skin had been alive beneath his hands, silky and sensual; her breast had fit the palm of his hand as if it was carved to match.

Damn it to hell! Hawk groaned, and looked down in disgust at his treacherous reaction to Sara Beaudry. *It's no use even dreaming fool,* he scolded himself. *She's just like the rest. She'll be gone when she's gotten what she came for . . . protection.*

He leaned over, turned off the hot water faucet, and blindly stepped into the full force of the icy spray. It did little to cool his aching body and he shivered as he exited his shower.

Hawk looked at his reflection in the cabinet mirror over the sink and frowned. Spinning about with decisive action, he grabbed a fresh towel from the linen shelf and quickly dried and dressed. He would have to face her, and it might as well be now. It wasn't going to get better between them until he did.

Hawk knocked on Sara's door, but received no invitation to enter. He knocked again and called, "Sara, come out and eat."

"I'm not hungry, thank you," she answered, a sarcastic drawl coloring her words.

"I didn't ask if you were hungry," Hawk said, his voice getting louder with each word, "I just said come eat, dammit!"

"You didn't say 'come eat dammit', you only said, 'come eat'," Sara said, flinging the door back dramatically and shoving the astounded man aside. "Had you said, 'come eat dammit' the first time, then, of course, I would have obeyed instantly because we all, *we, being women in general,*" she drawled, waving her arms about and hurling herself down the hall toward the kitchen, "know that when a man curses a command it must be obeyed instantly at all costs. Why? Because . . . because after that, he has no vocabulary left and must then resort to violence and we want, *I'm referring to women in general again,* to avoid violence at all costs. So . . ." she turned and nailed Hawk to the floor in stunned silence with her stare, "What's to eat?"

"Did Roger ever win an argument with you?" Hawk mumbled.

"Not ever!"

"Didn't think so," he muttered. Finding his footing and slipping past her, he cast a baleful eye her way, watching for a possible knife in his back as he passed. "Come on, little Wildcat," he coaxed. "I'll teach you how to make chili, mountain-style."

"I thought we were out of hamburger," Sara accused, following him into the kitchen. She hadn't forgiven, nor forgotten this morning. It was merely put on hold while her taste buds were being revitalized.

"We are. This is made from deer meat." He slipped a bit of a smile past Sara's vengeful stare and when she didn't slap it off his face, tried a full-fledged grin. "You haven't had good chili until you've had some of this."

When the smells of cumin, chili powder, and cooking meat had soaked through every starving pore of Sara's body and her stomach could wait no longer, she barged past Hawk, took the ladle he was using to stir the chili and dipped herself a steaming bowl of the food. She sat down to eat, ignoring Hawk's deadly grin.

"It's hot!" she shrieked, and dashed for the refrigerator, popping the top on the first can of liquid she touched. It happened to be beer, but it could have been mud for all she cared, as long as it put out the fire in her mouth and down her throat. She glared at Hawk over the top of the can and swallowed the cooling drink.

"Of course, it's hot, lady. You took the chili from a bubbling pot."

"Not hot like that, mister," she accused, and breathed loudly through her open mouth. "Hot with spices." She eyed the innocent looking bowl of food sitting in front of her and took another gulp of the beer.

"Why, Sara, I had no idea you were so delicate. I just assumed everyone from Texas ate chili like this. You know, Tex-Mex style." His words were as sarcastic as his smile.

"Yes . . . well," she mumbled, eyed the chili again, took the rest of the six-pack of beer from the refrigerator, and placed it directly before her. She popped the top of another can and set it in readiness beside her bowl as she took the second bite. By the time the bowl was empty, Sara was sloshed and Hawk was beginning to worry. Sara sober was enough for any one man to cope with. Sara drunk was another matter entirely. This may have been the biggest mistake of his life.

Sara was still hungry. One hunger had been satisfied, but watching Hawk move about the kitchen while she ate had fueled a different kind of hunger, and chili wasn't going to help.

"It's very warm in here, isn't it?"

Sara was having a problem with her eyes and blinked several times like a baby owl before she got them in focus.

"It's the chili, Sara, not the room temperature."

Hawk watched, leery of her stillness. For Sara it was unnatural.

"That and the fact you're loaded," Hawk muttered under his breath. He finished putting the kitchen to rights and stepped outside to feed Dog. When he came back inside, Sara was nowhere in sight.

"Great!" he muttered. He flipped the lights out, left the kitchen, and headed for Sara's bedroom, believing she may have become sick from a combination of no food, then too much chili and beer.

A shadowy figure standing still and silent in the middle of the living room floor stopped his search, and very nearly his heart.

"Damn! You scared me, Sara. What are you doing in the dark?" He reached for the light switch.

"Don't turn on the light . . . please." Her voice was soft, beckoning . . . promising.

"Sara, are you all right?" Hawk asked, and felt the room close in around him as she sighed softly into the darkness.

The quiet voice of the radio announcer filled the room as he introduced the next song of the evening. The music was country, sad and slow, and the beat matched the beat of Hawk's heart.

"Dance with me, Hawk."

Sara's whisper pulled him toward her into the darkened room, lit only by a light from upstairs spilling weakly out of a partially opened door.

"Sara," Hawk groaned. Caution slowed his footsteps, but not his blood as it raced through his veins and thickened his speech. He could barely think, let alone talk. He watched her sway to the beat of the music, her body moving like hot, sweet honey, as the tempo increased. Hawk knew she wouldn't be like this if she hadn't drunk so much beer, and she was going to be madder than hell in the morning if this didn't stop now. But, heaven help him, he didn't think he would if he could.

Then her voice beckoned again, this time mere inches away from his face.

"Dance with me, Hawk," she pleaded.

Less than the width of his hand separated them and Hawk could barely hear the music over the heartbeat pounding wildly in his ears.

"Witch," he whispered against her hair, and pulled her

into his arms, following the sway of her body to the music like a blind man follows sound.

Sara sighed, complete as his arms slid around her and held her close.

I'm dying, Hawk thought, *and I don't even care. Why after all these years do I find someone like you, Sara? Why didn't I know you first?* Hawk nested her fragility against the hard strength of his frame. *She fits my body like the other half of a puzzle,* Hawk thought. He splayed his hand across the hip pocket of her jeans and pulled her close against him, needing her softness to soothe a swollen ache. That's what he felt like, one giant ache.

Sara leaned back, looking up at him in the darkness, and pushed the lower half of her body hard against Hawk. He braced her with his other hand as she swayed ever so slightly. Sara slid her arms upward around his neck, and her hands into his hair, her fingers tangling in the silky, jet length. She pulled slowly at the back of his neck, urging him to claim all she offered.

Sara knew she was drunk, but knew what she was doing. It had only released her inhibitions and given desire free rein. She hurt so badly she didn't believe she could walk to save her soul. No one had ever said desire hurt. They had mentioned losing control, but never pain. She moved slowly against Hawk's lower body and the hard bulge behind his zipper made the pain worse . . . and better.

"Sara," Hawk warned, watching her every move as if his life depended on it. He caught his breath and felt her pushing up and against him, moving back and forth in time to the music until he felt he would burst.

This had gotten out of control too fast. Hawk wasn't sure he could stop, yet he knew he had to. Sara didn't know what she was doing and he wouldn't either if she didn't stop this madness.

"Honey, no!" Hawk ordered and tried to pull her arms from around his neck. But Sara tightened her grip and pulled him gently toward her slightly parted lips. Hawk felt the earth open and swallow him whole as he tasted Sara on his lips; felt the softness of her breasts against the rapid beat of his heart.

"No, baby!" he groaned, and then grabbed her arms and pushed her sharply away while still holding her at arm's length. His breath came in short, hard gasps as he tried to regain a measure of sanity.

"Not like this, little Wildcat, not like this. When we make love . . . and we will make love," his deep voice promised and wrapped around her last bit of good sense, "I want you wide awake and sober. I want you to see; I want you to feel. I'll make you sorry it's over and crazy for more. But not now, honey. Not now."

Sara leaned her head weakly into his chest, clutched the fabric of his shirt in desperation and whispered thickly as she swallowed back tears.

"I'm already sober, Mackenzie Hawk, and I'm already sorry. I'm sorry it was over before it began."

Hawk watched her gather her wits about her and walk from the room like a slightly tipsy queen.

Somewhere in the hills a wolf howled and close by Hawk's dog answered the mournful call. The first flakes of the promised snow fell silently on the roof and onto the ground. By morning, all would be frozen again on the Kiamichi. Sara snuggled deeply under her covers and dreamed of an angel, all bronze and gold, who flew too low to the earth and crashed into her heart.

Hawk dreamed not at all, but sat at the fireside and

watched the dance of the flames, like the flames in his heart, hot and high and burning into ashes.

"I've located the position of your merchandise, sir. However, there is a hitch. It's in the mountains, just as I suspected, but an extremely heavy snowfall and inaccessible roads prevent travel at this time. No . . . there shouldn't be any problem there, sir. Only one man is watching her and he seems to be a local. You know, long hair, outdoor type of man. No, I don't know his name yet, but I doubt it matters. He looks to be some mountain-type Indian, I think."

Silence filled the phone booth and the glass began to fog over from the tracker's breath as he listened, stunned by possibilities he hadn't covered. If his employer's warning was to be heeded, he had indeed bitten off a larger hunk than he could chew and swallow alone. This news could delay retrieval of the merchandise but might insure success . . . and he did thrive on success.

He hung up the receiver, surprised that his employer had taken the news of the delay so well. In fact, he had seemed . . . excited. Even offered to join him and help in the retrieval. The tracker didn't mind as long as his fee remained the same. However, according to his employer, the guard had skills he hadn't counted on. Therefore, a bit of alteration was necessary.

Tracker dug absently into his pockets and smiled as he pulled out the treat. The Tootsie Roll wrapper fell unheeded to the floor of the phone booth as the tracker stepped out onto the dimly-lit street corner in Broken Bow. His cheeks sank in as he sucked noisily on the candy and hummed a tuneless melody while walking away. *When this job is over, I think I'll take a trip to Bermuda where it's warm and sunny. I hate all this damn wind and snow,* he thought. *Hell, maybe I'll even retire.*

SIX

Nearly a foot of snow had fallen during the night and more was coming down with no promise of ceasing. An ominous silence filled the cabin and the two inhabitants went about the business of unnecessary chores simply to stay out of each other's way. Hawk was uneasy about what Sara might remember from the night before. He'd said more than he meant to and less than he could have. He regretted his lapse because he needed his thoughts strictly on the job at hand. He had a gut feeling things would not stay in limbo much longer. Levette had a very thorough network of informants. Hawk feared the only reason he and Sara were still undetected was due entirely to the fresh snowfall and inaccessible roads. For once, he was grateful Old Woman had insisted on living so far away and so high on the Kiamichi. It may be all that would save their lives.

Sara paced. Every menial, piddly job she could find had been done. She had washed and dried her hair, cleaned already sparkling rooms, and done all her laundry, which didn't consist of much, thanks to her limited wardrobe of three changes of sweatshirts, jeans, and one oversize T-shirt. She was out of makeup and couldn't care less. She surmised the uglier she looked, the uglier she would feel, and maybe give herself something else to think about besides making love to Mackenzie Hawk. She might be crazy, but she wasn't a masochist and this relationship seemed to be a lost cause. *Fine!* she fumed. *There's plenty more to worry about besides wondering how it would feel to lie naked, ivory to mahogany, skin to skin, as close as* . . . Sara gasped aloud at her own thoughts and muttered under her breath, "Stop! Stop it now, you fool. Someone wants me dead and all I can do is lust after this pigheaded Indian."

Sara silently scolded herself and increased her speed as she walked from window to window throughout the cabin, on lookout, waiting for whatever terror the future promised.

"Do we have guards?" Sara asked.

Hawk jumped and pivoted to find Sara staring point blank, her expression demanding an answer. He was surprised she hadn't asked earlier, since she was so fond of being in control. He answered instantly, without his usual reticence, and vaguely surprised himself. Sara Beaudry was good for him.

"Yes. The Colonel stationed your brother's squad of men in position when he left." He knew Sara's next concern would be the bad weather and their comforts, so he continued. "They are well-trained in survival techniques and have enough camping equipment. Also, there is another thing you should know." He beckoned her to follow him upstairs. Once there, he opened his closet door and pushed aside several articles of clothing.

"Feel here, Sara." Hawk took her hand in his and

guided it down the satin smooth finish of the cedar-lined closet. "There, just a bit to the right, below the darkest whorl in the wood. Now, press it. Harder," he commanded.

Sara gasped as a panel swung open, revealing a tiny enclosure. Inside were some lethal-looking handguns, electrical equipment, detonating devices, and a hand-held radio complete with antennae and a tiny light that emitted a steady, consistent flash.

"I didn't turn in all my gear when summer camp was over," Hawk drawled, pulling the radio out into the light.

"I'll bet you steal towels from hotels, too," Sara grinned. They looked sheepishly at each other, surprised at how easily they kept falling back into a comfortable relationship.

"What is this for?" she asked, focusing on the flashing light.

"All you need to do to summon help is press this button," he pointed to the object in question, "and it will instantly activate a distress signal. The light will stop flashing, giving out a steady beam instead. The men on guard are experts, Sara. They'll be here in minutes."

"Okay, now I know," Sara drawled, a shaky quality in her speech that she was obviously trying to mask. "You signal for help when we see them coming."

"Sara, pay attention. If anything happens to me, you have to signal for help immediately. Levette will show you no mercy."

Seeing the stricken look in her eyes, he quipped, "If you can't get to the radio, just feed them some of your hamburger recipes."

Sara refused to be sidetracked. As she watched Hawk carefully place the radio back in its hiding place and close the panel, she spoke, her voice shaking as she whispered.

"Nothing is going to happen to you. Nothing! Do you hear me, it can't."

Hawk took hold of her shoulders and shook her gently, trying to impress Sara of the seriousness of the situation. "Yes, it can, baby. Be realistic. Your life may depend on it."

"No . . . no!" she cried. "It can't, I tell you."

Hawk was surprised at Sara's reaction. She always seemed level-headed, even hard-headed; this hysterical reaction was out of character.

"Sara, I'm not immortal. What's wrong with you?" He tried in vain to comfort her distress and her answer nearly broke his heart.

"If anything happens to you, it will be my fault. My fault for coming here and for involving you in this . . . this . . . nightmare. I can't live with that." Her whole body was shaking as she pressed a hand to her lips, trying to stifle the scream she felt crawling up her throat. "I couldn't live knowing you had died because of me. I wouldn't want to."

Sara stumbled out of the closet and down the stairs. Her mind in shock at the words she'd just uttered. She hadn't known she was going to say that until the words had fallen from her lips. Just the thought of being alive, breathing, going about the daily business of living with Mackenzie Hawk not on the same earth was unthinkable. He didn't have to be with her. He didn't even have to like her. But he did have to be somewhere on earth, under the same sky, breathing the same air. She had to have that much from life.

Sara sank limply upon a windowseat overlooking the blinding whiteness of the meadow in front of the cabin, yet she saw none of the cold beauty. She trembled and her teeth chattered, but she wasn't cold, she was afraid.

She was afraid because she loved Mackenzie Hawk. She loved him and he was never going to love her back.

She buried her head in her hands and let all the fear, all the loneliness, all the heartache overwhelm her. She was so tired of fighting. She was tired of being brave . . . just plain tired.

"Nothing is ever going to be right again," she whispered to herself.

"Yes, it will, baby." Hawk gently touched the top of her bowed head, aching for the fear and confusion he couldn't take away.

Sara jumped. She didn't realize she'd spoken aloud until Hawk had answered.

"Soon this will all be over. It'll be nothing but a bad dream. You'll be back in Dallas before you know it." Just voicing those words made him crazy. *But*, he thought, *that's where she belongs.*

"It hasn't all been bad, Hawk," Sara whispered, and cradled the side of his face with her hand, her eyes searching his face for some sign of hope for her useless dreams. And then she whispered softly against his cheek as she pressed her lips gently upon a muscle that twitched uncontrollably, betraying the extreme emotion Hawk struggled to hide. "Some of it is what dreams are made of." With those words eating into his soul, Hawk stood silently and watched Sara slip away and walk slowly into the kitchen.

His heart ached, his arms ached to cradle her, he ached in places he'd just as soon forget. And he could only just imagine how afraid she must be; how foreign this upheaval and uncertainty. He had lived this kind of life so long, it was a part of him, part of why he accepted no favors and trusted no one. In his experience, there had been few to trust. He wanted to take Sara and hide her forever from all the evil and the hurt the world had to offer. But Sara would have none of that. She was all beauty and trust and light, and Hawk knew light couldn't be hidden. He couldn't hide Sara like he'd hidden himself. She wasn't going to let him.

It was nearly dusk. Hawk sighed, dusted off his gloves, and took a breather from hauling in extra firewood. The night temperatures promised a below-zero wind chill, and he wanted to keep the fireplace well supplied. The circulating heat system that serviced the cabin worked well only if the fire in the fireplace kept burning, and that meant lots of wood.

Dog came running out of the trees bordering the cabin clearing and barked a greeting. Hawk grinned, watching Dog jump from one virgin snowdrift to another, leaving a huge imprint of his bulky body within each one as he bounded toward him. He suspected there wasn't a rabbit within three miles of the cabin that hadn't been chased today from the looks of his pet.

He whistled, stepped down from the porch and held out his arms as Dog pounced on his chest. It was an old game they played, they wrestled about in the snow, but finally Hawk had to call a halt. He was dripping wet from the snow melting on his overheated body and chilling from the clammy feel of his soaked clothing.

"Enough, boy. Down! Down! Once again, old boy, you win." Laughter and exertion blended together and gave a rarely heard lilt to his voice.

Sara stood in the doorway watching Hawk play with such abandon. The cold breeze blew dark hair roughly about his face and his eyes sparkled and glowed; alive with laughter and the pure joy of living.

He is so much man, Sara thought, as she watched Hawk play with Dog. *But he lives in such a lonely, solitary state. Why?* she wondered. *Why would someone choose this existence when . . .*

Sara caught her breath. A thought just occurred to her. He lives here by necessity, not choice. It can't cost much to live alone, heat with firewood cut from one's own land, and eat game harvested from one's own land. She also suspected he hadn't worked at a paying job since he quit the Company. As far as she knew, he had no job at all.

Great! This makes it even harder. He doesn't trust women. He's probably broke. He'll never accept anything from me. He won't accept my love, he damn sure won't accept money. What am I going to do now? She groaned and leaned her head against the door window in frustration, watching her breath fog up the scene before her eyes until Hawk and Dog were mere misty ghosts. A lone tear slipped down her cheek in silent frustration.

Hawk's ability, or inability to pay his way in society was not what drew Sara Beaudry. It was the man himself that was so addictive. And like a true addict, Sara could no more stay away from Hawk than she could quit breathing. She didn't care about money. She only cared about Hawk.

She opened the door and stepped out onto the back porch just as Hawk called a halt to his game.

"Trade you places, Dog," Sara said, trying to hide the longing in her voice with a teasing note.

Hawk turned, breathing heavily from exertion, and vainly tried to slow the beat of his pounding heart by gulping huge draughts of the icy air. Dog barked once as if bidding adieu and bounded back into the forest. He disappeared quickly in the fast-fading light of day.

Hawk read the look in Sara's eyes as easily as he read tracks in the forest. She was hurting. He knew what would make her pain go away, but feared in the long run it would merely be replaced by a greater one if he didn't leave Sara . . . and well enough . . . alone. But dear God, he was tempted.

"Don't, Sara," he murmured, his voice deep and ragged. He stood still, watching her face transformed by his rejection; just another of the many since they'd been together.

There was only one option Sara had left besides beg and cry, which she totally refused to consider, and so she chose it—anger.

"Don't what, Hawk?" she cried, derision and anger flying at him in the darkness. "Don't touch? Don't laugh? Don't cry? Don't care?" Her voice shook with suppressed tears and her words came thickly as they struggled past the choking lump in her throat. "You may as well ask me not to breathe. It would be easier."

They stood facing each other in the darkness; Sara's last words echoing in the night air. Hawk bore her chastisement with a heavy heart, yet there was nothing he could say that would ease her.

"Damn you, Mackenzie Hawk. Damn you for making this so hard." Sara swallowed a sob as she continued. "You're such a fool. It's so easy to love, Hawk. So easy. All you have to do is care . . . and I know you care. But . . ." And her voice shook as she whispered her accusation, "You also have to trust. You asked me to trust you and I did, unequivocally. It's a real shame you can't return the favor."

She turned and disappeared into the cabin, slamming the door behind her, leaving Hawk alone in the night with her accusations ringing in his ears. Her words had pushed Hawk as close to the breaking point as he'd ever been. Then something occurred to him as he silently accepted

Sara's accusations. It wasn't true he didn't trust her. It was himself he didn't trust.

He shivered, suddenly very cold and aware of his surroundings, and walked slowly up the steps and into the cabin. He removed his wet clothing in the backroom, moving like an automaton while performing the routine chore.

Habits Old Woman had instilled in him at an early age were still with Hawk, although she was not. She had insisted work clothing be left at the back entry, instead of tracking and dripping throughout the home. A change of clothes or a robe was always hanging on clothes pegs, ready for the user to wear. Hawk absently reached for the fresh clothing and came up with air.

Sara must have washed everything in sight, he thought, and stepped into the kitchen, reaching into the depths of the clothes dryer, hoping for at least a bath towel, but no such luck. She'd done her job well. He shrugged and sighed. Delay was only chilling him more, so he padded on bare feet through the darkened rooms, hoping to gain the safety of his room unseen. More than halfway up the stairs, he heard sounds from below that bore investigation.

It sounded like Sara was in the process of renovating the entire downstairs. He suspected one of her fits was in progress and he was the cause. He took the rest of the stairs two at a time, reached around the corner of the door to his bedroom and grabbed a pair of Levis, soft and faded from countless washings. He stepped into the soft, clinging legs of faded denim, ignored his shirt, and bolted back down the stairs.

Hurrying through the living room and down the long hallway to Sara's room, Hawk took a deep breath and then threw open the door to her room to be greeted by chaos. Sara hadn't touched a thing in the room that had belonged to Old Woman, but she had pulled everything she'd brought with her, plus the few items Hawk had purchased for her, and had them scattered in disarray on the bed and dresser. A huge shoulder bag lay open upon the bed and Sara was frantically jamming clothing and toilet articles alike into its depths.

Sara heard the door hit the wall, but didn't spare Hawk a glance as she continued banging drawers and doors.

"What in hell do you think you're doing?" Hawk demanded, fear making his words harsher than intended.

"Get out!" Sara yelled, anger and frustration evident as she flung belongings about in wild abandon.

Hawk grabbed her roughly and spun her about to face him. Had she any sense left at the time, she would have been petrified by the expression on his face, but she was too far gone to notice, or care.

"I asked you a question," he said, his words low and guttural, and took hold of her shoulders and shook her, trying to force an answer from her hysteria.

Her hair tumbled down from its loose topknot and fell about her face and shoulders, covering Hawk's hand like a blanket of fire. He shook her again, desperation in his actions, and her head fell back, bumping against the paneling on the wall. He pinned her roughly with his body, putting himself between her and the doorway.

Sara thrust her chin forward, defying Hawk in the only way he'd left open and muttered angrily, "I'm leaving, mister. I'm getting out of your hair . . . out of your way . . . out of your life. You can signal Roger. He'll be here in minutes, and then your miserable life will be right back where it was before I ever entered it. You stay on this mountain, you hide from me, or from anyone or anything that might make you feel. I don't care anymore. Do you hear me? I don't care!"

The instant the last syllable was out of her mouth, she

knew she'd gone too far, but it was too late to call back her words. The look on his face, the look in his eyes. Sara began to shake. She struggled weakly, trying to wrench herself free from his hold. Her eyes widened and she caught back a gasp, suddenly aware of Hawk's state of mind and . . . undress.

Oh, God! Sara thought and closed her eyes, swallowing back the bitter taste of anger as another, more subtle emotion overcame her . . . Desire.

"You aren't going anywhere." He whispered his terse command against her face.

Sara could feel the heat of his breath against her closed eyelids.

"Hawk, please," she pleaded, feeling his near-naked body pressing closer and closer against her. She felt the power of him, and the need in him

"Please what, little Wildcat?" And when all he got for an answer was her sharply indrawn breath, he ordered, "Sara, look at me. Open your eyes and look at me."

His command was impossible to deny. His body demanded as his words cajoled. Sara opened her eyes, met his look and fell into a world of green, all hot and humid, like the endless depths of a tropical rain forest.

"Touch me," he whispered.

And her hands obeyed, sliding up the hard, ropey muscles of his arms and shoulders and across his chest. She could feel the wild, rapid beat of his heart that lay encased in a chest of copper-colored steel. She watched his pupils dilate and his nostrils flare as her hands slid lower, down past a hard, lean waist, past the unbuttoned waistband of his Levis, and lower.

Sara closed her eyes again and leaned her forehead against his bare chest, inhaling the very essence of him while letting her lips graze the taut skin covering iron muscles and a heartbeat that echoed in her mind like a war-drum tattoo.

Hawk held his breath, dying a little with each inch of skin she touched, hoping, praying, shuddering with need as her searching fingers traveled lower and lower, until his control snapped and sent sanity into another dimension. This world . . . his world . . . consisted of Sara, only Sara, and nothing else mattered.

His mouth clung to her lips, drawing her sweetness into him in huge, life-giving draughts. His hands shook as he pressed the lower half of his aching body into her hips, letting her cradle the need that was driving him wild. Hawk slid his hands under Sara's sweatshirt, up, up, slowly, slowly, until they reached their goal.

Sara leaned into Hawk's searching hands, seeking relief from the intensity of emotion that was flooding her being. The rough, calloused tips of Hawk's fingers searched and teased, making her body feel swollen, heavy, yet her breath came in gasps too quick to count.

"Sara," Hawk murmured. His voice coaxed as his hands seduced, yet he couldn't entice Sara to open her eyes. *But you will, little Wildcat,* Hawk thought, as his hands moved over her body; his lips working their sweet torture on the tender curve of her cheeks and down the gentle slope of her neck.

His head dipped lower as he tasted the swell of her breasts before venturing into the valley between to stake his claim. Hawk filled his hands with her breasts, taking a swollen nub between each thumb and forefinger and smiled slowly to himself, watching Sara's eyelids flutter weakly as a small, quiet moan escaped from between her slightly parted lips.

Sara felt all the blood in her body rushing toward the center of her being. She was no longer in control of her thoughts, her body, her soul. It all belonged to Mackenzie Hawk and the magic he was working on her heart.

Hawk was nearly past the point of sanity himself, and reacted with pure instinct as Sara's head fell weakly against his arm. He caught her roughly against him just as the remaining strength ebbed from her shaky legs. A fierce, wild gleam of joy pierced the armor of his heart. There would be no more waiting.

Suddenly it was quiet, and all she could hear were the sounds of breaths being drawn through tortured lungs. Sara opened her eyes and the sight she saw nearly stopped her heart.

"Help me," Sara begged.

Her plea was obeyed as a low growl slid from between Hawk's tightly clinched jaw.

Sara felt his hands tear at her clothing and it fell unheeded to the floor, felt his hands on her body, felt the wild pulse of his heart match the rhythm of her own. Their blood ran hot and high on the Kiamichi. She was lost in the heat of his gaze, hypnotized by the strength of his need, drawn to his desperation.

She felt herself lifted from the floor and then held suspended for a second before Hawk lowered her onto the pulsing thrust of his body.

Sara gasped, realizing what Hawk had done, and moaned softly as he slid deeper and deeper into her. The sensation was maddening.

Hawk took a deep, shaky breath, willing himself to control the blinding need to thrust hard and wild.

He couldn't take his eyes from Sara's face. Her gaze was fixed, staring straight into his soul. Her lips parted in a sigh when he shifted position, moving himself deeper into her warmth. Her head lolled back against the wall; the sensation more than Sara could bear. Hawk slid both arms around her slender body to protect her fragile skin from the hard, polished surface of the paneling.

"Come here, baby," he urged, and she obeyed by wrapping her legs about Hawk's body and her arms about his neck.

Sara braced herself against the wall and felt the cushion of his hands at her back. Desperation set in as Hawk stayed virtually motionless within her. Sara's hunger and a need for completion was building to near unbearable heights and still he did not move. She ached for the thrust, the movement that would take away this craving that threatened to consume her. Her body felt his presence, felt his need growing as he swelled within her until she feared she could not contain him, and still he would not move. He was going to make her beg.

Sara moaned, a low, aching cry Hawk could no longer ignore, and he leaned forward, and ever so gently, flicked the tip of his tongue across her lips, tracing the line of her mouth with it as he tasted her sweetness.

Her breath came in sharp, quick gasps. Hawk felt tiny tremors convulsing about his manhood and could barely control the need to drive himself deep, losing control and himself in the sweet, sweet warmth of Sara.

"Oh, God!" Sara begged. "No more, Hawk, please, please. I ache. I hurt. Make it stop . . . only you can make it stop . . . please." Tears ran freely down her face and she closed her eyes as a wave of desire swept over her so fiercely, she feared she would faint. Her eyelids fluttered weakly and she shook with a need that was driving her insane.

"Open your eyes, Sara. You look at me . . . look at me good. I want you to watch me, sweet baby. I'm going to teach you how to fly."

Sara obeyed. Hawk moved and she felt his massive

strength gather her close against him. Then, finally, God help her, he took her hard and fast and sent her falling, falling, into his heat, into the fire, and then heard his voice from far away calling her back, back into his arms. And they soared, high and free on the Kiamichi.

Sara vaguely remembered being carried to Hawk's eryie, and being laid ever so gently in a bed of satin and down. A surprise, this sensual side of Mackenzie Hawk, sleeping on down-filled, satin comforters, but the thought was soon put aside in the heat of Hawk's unleashed passion. Over and over, into the night and the coming morning, Hawk took Sara to the brink of insanity, driving her into a blinding need for satisfaction that only he could provide. Once he'd tasted, he could not get enough of Sara. He'd known it would be like that with them. Maybe that was why he had hesitated so long. Finally, they fell into an exhausted sleep, wrapped in a tangle of arms and legs and satin, unwilling to part, even in slumber.

Sara had been watching him sleep for hours. She had reveled in the opportunity to study this man, Mackenzie Hawk, who had stolen her heart. However, she was still just the least bit uncertain what he planned to do with his stolen treasure. But she no longer doubted Hawk's feelings for her. It hadn't been mere lust and proximity that had been responsible for last night.

He could write a book, Sara thought; remembering the ecstasy he'd brought her to, time and again, with little thought for his own satisfaction. Sara had little experience on which to base her comparison, but Hawk was like no other man she'd ever known. Wildly and fiercely, he had claimed her and then loved her with a tender, generous gentleness that had nearly broken her heart.

He looked younger, more approachable, as he lay wrapped in the mound of bedclothes and Sara. The morning sunlight gave his skin a burnished, copper glow and his hair lay like black silk against the pillow and across Sara's outstretched hand. She fanned her fingers, allowing his hair to fall through the spaces like midnight falling through the crack of dawn. His lips were firm and cool, but slightly swollen from the past night's passion and Sara frowned as she ran a delicate finger across their chiseled perfection.

So much hurt, so much pain inside him; please, God, he'll let me take it all away.

Sara sighed and moved closer, pillowing her head against his massive chest. She smiled to herself as she felt his arms tighten. Even asleep he wouldn't let her go.

Hawk was dreaming. He stood under the bright-blue Oklahoma sky and watched Sara running toward him. Her mouth was parted in a silent scream. His heart raced and his feet twitched, but he stood rooted to the ground as Sara called his name over and over in the light of day. He held out his hand, beckoning her near, yet no matter how fast she ran, she never came any closer. And then he saw the other man, laughing and screaming as he drew closer and closer to Sara. Levette! It was Levette! Hawk could see him clearly now. The tall, slender build, blonde wavy hair and wideset brown eyes that were hard and empty, like burned-out coals in the face of a devil. Beauty and cruelty blended in such a manner was somehow an abomination of nature. It had overcome itself in the physical perfection and completely forgotten about a conscience or soul.

Sara! Sara! Look out! Hawk called, but she did not hear and Levette drew even closer. Hawk moaned and tossed, the tangle of bedclothes weighing him down. From the frozen nightmare, he watched in horror as Sara finally reached his arms and safety. He saw her smile, saw the love and trust in her eyes vanish just as Levette laughed and pulled the trigger.

Hawk jumped and sat straight up in bed, his heart pounding as sweat poured off his body like tears.

"You were dreaming," Sara said, reaching out to comfort him. She'd not been aware of his unrest until he'd moaned and called her name aloud as he slept.

"A dream," he muttered, and wiped a shaky hand across his face. "Jesus! Come here, baby. I need to hold you."

He gathered her gently into his arms and held her cradled against his chest.

Sara could feel the wild beat of his heart and she splayed her fingers across his chest, trying to soothe its frantic flight.

"Sara, love me," he pleaded, and pulled her across his lap, her legs on either side of his waist.

Sara faced him; a viking queen with auburn hair and ivory skin wrapped around his growing need, giving as well as taking from her liege lord. She pulled his head toward her and pillowed it on her breasts.

Hawk moaned and buried his face in the twin perfections. Then moving gently, he took a delicate rose-tipped breast into his mouth and nibbled and stroked it until the nub was hard and swollen and aching for relief. But relief was not in sight, for he turned instead and brought its twin to matching attention.

"Hawk, darling, please let me," Sara begged. She kissed the top of his head and down the side of his face before he claimed her lips and took the breath from her body. His arms tightened spasmodically before he sighed and relinquished the hold on his woman: that was how he thought of Sara and had for longer than he would admit. Right or wrong, she was now his woman. Hawk acquiesced at her pleadings and lay back in the tangle of satin, allowing Sara's request.

With tenderness and love in every movement and touch, Sara teased and caressed, bringing Hawk to an intensity nearly beyond bearing before she lifted herself and slid slowly onto his aching manhood. She paused a moment, allowing herself time to fit to his body then leaned over, brushing the nipples of his chest with the curtain of her hair. Sara couldn't believe Hawk had allowed her this much control. He was showing her the only way he could of his trust and need for her.

This giving of love was so much more than the taking. Rocking slowly and then with increasing tempo as their bodies joined in an ancient dance of love, they came to completion. Then, laughing aloud with infectious pleasure, they drifted slowly back into a light slumber, warm and replete.

"Hawk, darling," Sara whispered, tracing the line of well-defined muscles across his chest.

He felt the touch, heard the teasing note in her voice and smiled. "Hmmmmm?" he answered, and wrapped his hand around and around a long length of her hair before tilting her head back gently with a tug as Sara rested her head on his shoulder.

She threw one of her long legs across the lower half of his body, pinning him with its weight as he pulled at her hair and urged her to finish her sentence.

"How long do you suppose it would take to starve to death if we never left this bed?"

Hawk took one look at the elfin grin on her face and

rolled over, pinning her under him with practiced finess. "What's the matter, little Wildcat, have I neglected your welfare?"

Sara's stomach growled loudly, embarrassing her and startling Hawk into rounds of deep, booming laughter. "Come on, baby. I think it's time reality reared its ugly head and we find sustenance. Someone told me you can't live on love alone, it's obviously true." He claimed her lips with a searing kiss that curled Sara's toes and straightened her hair before bounding out of their bed and walking toward the shower, unconcerned with his unclad state.

As Sara watched his bare backside disappear into the bathroom, she almost forgot she was hungry. Sara fell from the tangled bedcovers and followed Hawk's retreat.

Thanks to a shared shower and lack of clothes, it was another couple of hours before Sara and Hawk found their way to the kitchen and even later still before they got any food cooked to eat.

The food scraps in Dog's pan are varied, to say the least, Hawk thought, as he stood on the back porch and scraped the remnants of their meal into the pan's icy surface. If he didn't get himself under control, they actually might starve to death, but only because their fire for each other burned faster than food cooked. This need was overwhelming and crazy . . . and dangerous . . . if he didn't pull himself together and worry about the situation at hand.

And worry he did because it looked like the snow was melting. That meant they would no longer be isolated. Safety was melting and running down the Kiamichi in icy rivulets. There was no more time for dreaming. The nightmare was at hand.

An owl flew overhead and landed in a tree by the cabin and Hawk shivered. It was unusual to see an owl in broad daylight and he had to fight back the fear that crawled down his back as he remembered one of Old Woman's beliefs.

Indian folklore had branded the owl as a messenger of death. It either represented coming death or the soul of a man already passing, Hawk couldn't remember which. Either way, it gave him reason to worry. More than he cared to admit of his Indian heritage clung to his rationale. The owl's eerie presence made him hurry indoors to Sara; to prepare her for what would be coming up the Kiamichi as the melted snow ran down.

The helicopter landed in the grassy pasture and four men spilled out of its belly like the offal of a gutted fish. That's what they were, society's dregs, moldering left-overs for hire to the man with the most money. One man stood aside as the other three gathered gear from the marshy grassland and melting snow. His blonde hair lay in wavy perfection on his head, glowing in the daylight like a halo. The perfection of his smile only increased the beauty of his face and countenance, and fooled Tracker who was hurrying toward the waiting men.

Then Tracker stopped, an unexplained chill making his bowels rattle as fear churned the depths of his stomach. It was only with the greatest of efforts that he controlled the urge to turn and run as he looked into the flat, emotion-less eyes of his employer. Swallowing nervously, he finally found his voice and spoke, his words shooting from his lips in quick, staccato bursts.

"This way, sir. I've rented a four-wheel drive truck. I believe it will maneuver quite well in this." He gestured, indicating the mud and snow and mushy ground underneath.

"It had better," the man threatened, pinning Tracker

with a forceful stare. "I've waited entirely too long for
. . . satisfaction." He smiled and rubbed himself suggestively. "And . . . as you are well aware . . . I *demand*
satisfaction."

SEVEN

Sara paused on the staircase and watched Hawk standing sentinel at the window. He was all long legs and narrow hips encased in a pair of black denim Levis, a red-and-black plaid shirt that accentuated the width of his shoulders and lean waist, and coal-black hair that hung loosely down the back of his collar to just above his shoulders.

He needs a haircut, Sara thought, and then her heart thumped one wild, erratic beat before it settled back into its regular rhythm. He was wearing a shoulder holster. Sara could see the wide leather strap, ominous by its mere presence. She fiddled with her hairbrush, debating whether or not to ask Hawk for the help she needed when he sensed her presence and turned to see her standing on the stairs.

"What is it, Sara?" his deep voice beckoned. Although he didn't need to ask, he knew what had stopped her descent.

"Do I need one?" she asked, trying to appear nonchalant.

Instantly, her referral to his being armed sparked such a fierce spurt of pride for her that he couldn't contain the smile that tilted a corner of his mouth.

"Can you shoot?" he asked.

"Ummm, no," Sara hesitated, still twisting her hairbrush over and over between trembling fingers.

"Then you don't need a gun, baby. Come here." He held out his arms and enfolded Sara safely against him.

She clutched at the front of his shirt, willing her fear away while held in his strength.

"What are you doing with that thing?" he teased, referring to the brush she still held clutched in one hand. "Going to turn the bad guys over your knee?" He grinned at her indignant expression.

"No, funny man. I have tangles I can't reach, no thanks to you and last night. Will you help?" She handed him the brush and turned her back to him, giving him easier access to the mess of curls.

Hawk dug his fingers into the tangle of her hair, entranced as auburn spirals lively wound about his hands and wrists. Reluctantly, he withdrew his hands, took the hairbrush and proceeded to coax the impudent curls into a semblance of manners, despite their preference for rebellion.

"Did you know today is Christmas Eve?" The wistful tone of her voice hinted at what she could not say.

"Are you sorry you're not in Dallas?" Hawk had to ask, although he dreaded her answer. Somewhere deep inside, he still doubted.

"There's no one there, Hawk. There hasn't been for the longest time. I only have Roger . . . and now you."

His hands stilled and he pulled her back against his body and buried his face in her hair.

Sara grabbed his arms and wrapped herself in his hug.

"I'm only sorry this is happening and you've become involved because of me. I would wish happier times for you at Christmas than babysitting a time bomb."

"No, Sara, you've got it all wrong. You are my happier times. I don't want to be anywhere else but here . . . with you."

"I do miss one thing," she said. "I miss the anticipation of Christmas. I really get into decorating and baking. I love to cook. I just rarely have the time to indulge myself."

"Yeah, you're a good cook, too, baby. What Christmas food can you make from hamburger?"

Sara grinned and spun about, sending the hairbrush flying across the room as she threw a playful punch at Hawk's midsection.

"Funny . . . real funny, big man." She grinned, watching the mischief dance in his eyes. *Dear Lord, I love to hear him laugh.* And before she talked herself out of it, she took a deep breath, wrapped her arms about his waist, laid her head against his heart and spoke. "This may not be an ideal way to spend Christmas, but I can't complain about the company I've been keeping. In a strange way, I'm glad all this happened because it brought me to you."

Hawk's arms tightened, pulling her closer against him, and it gave Sara the impetus to continue.

"Thank you for the best Christmas present I've ever received," Sara said, turning her face to his puzzled gaze.

"Baby, I didn't give you anything except a hard time . . . and a place to hide." Hawk's voice was low and regretful.

"Yes, you did, Mackenzie Hawk. You gave me love."

Hawk was stunned. Too moved to speak, he saw the truth shining on her face and could not deny her. He shook his head, emotion overwhelming his speech.

"Sara." The name came out like a prayer. Hawk swallowed, trying to speak past a strange thickening in his throat. Nothing more would come past his lips but her name as he looked at love through a curtain of tears.

He stepped backward to the windowseat and pulled her down onto his lap. Words were beyond him, but touching was not as Sara received the sweetest kiss she would ever know.

"Merry Christmas, my love," Sara whispered, as Hawk drew her into his arms.

They turned back to the window and reality; the job of sentinel once again a necessity.

Sara took a load of sheets from the clothes dryer. She had to stay busy or go stark raving mad.

"Hawk," she called as she started upstairs, "I'm putting fresh sheets on your bed, okay?"

Hawk had cautioned Sara so many times, it was now second nature to check in as she moved from room to room.

He grinned and nodded as he watched her rear view disappearing up the stairs. She was just as sexy going as coming. Then he noticed the wood supply by the fireplace was running low and went toward the back door to replenish the stack. Waiting until dark to navigate the back porch steps with armfuls of wood was not wise, especially with Levette still on the loose.

Hawk opened the door and took a deep, refreshing breath of the cold mountain air. Normally, he was outside most of the daylight hours and missed the activity. But Sara's safety and this situation had altered his routine.

Hawk grunted. He always got about one stick too much wood, but couldn't control the urge to lessen the number of trips by enlarging the quantity of wood hauled at each time. It was never a good idea, but he couldn't seem to break the habit. He was trying to balance the armload of wood and almost missed the bit of paper blowing across the muddy yard. It caught briefly in the woodpile before dancing its way across the yard and into the forest. He wondered absently how in the world a candy wrapper had gotten so far up the mountain. Tootsie Rolls were kids candies and no one he knew up the mountain had any . . . Hawk stopped instantly. Everything he knew about Levette told him he was here. He felt his presence, could almost smell the evil. Hawk spun about; his eyes cold jade searching the treeline. Still holding his load of firewood, he felt the impact of the bullet slam into the wood a heartbeat after he heard the shot. The force of the shot from the high-powered weapon knocked the wood from his arms and Hawk flat on his back. Precious seconds were wasted as he struggled to catch his breath and when he could, it came out in a groan.

It felt like he'd cracked a rib. The second bullet ploughed into the ground inches from his face, sending a spray of mud into the air, but Hawk was already rolling underneath the crawl space beneath his back porch.

Sara heard the sound, like a frozen branch cracking under the weight of too much ice and snow, but when the second followed so quickly, her heart stopped. Rifle shots! She ran to the only window in the room, yet saw nothing but endless trees and melting snow.

"Oh, God, no!" she whispered. "It's started," and forced back the urge to run. "Please, Lord, let Hawk be all right. Anything you ask of me, anything, just let him live."

Sara repeated her prayer over and over; a litany of promise, as she ran to his closet and frantically shoved hangers of clean clothing aside, searching for the hidden panel.

There, no! Damn, damn, damn. Where is that place? She was shaking so badly, she could hardly concentrate. She ran her hand wildly up and down the smooth cedar walls, frantically searching for the spot that would spring open the panel so she could activate the distress signal. *Thank you, Lord*, she thought, as it sprung back, revealing the nest of weapons and the object of her search. *There, it's done*. The beam of light stopped flashing and began emitting instead one steady pulse of light. *It was working!*

Only seconds had lapsed from the time Sara heard the shots until she'd activated the radio signal, but it felt like hours. She stood motionless in the center of the room, listening. She was terrified. She wanted Hawk; to hear him coming up the stairs laughing, telling her it was a mistake and Roger was probably going to throttle her for the false alarm. Yet she heard nothing but the beat of her heart. She didn't know what to do. If she went in search of Hawk as she so desperately wanted, it might make matters worse. But . . . he could be lying in the cold; bleeding to death and nothing could be worse than that.

Please, God. Just let Roger come soon, and she sank limply against the side of the bed and waited for a sign.

Hawk struggled around in the cramped space, trying to get his pistol out of its holster. It hurt to breath. He closed his eyes for a few seconds and concentrated, willing himself to calm down; slowing his heartbeat to a constant, calculated thud.

The porch steps prevented him from a clear view of the trees where the shots had originated. But they also protected him from further attack and he needed the edge. He watched, eyes trained for any movement, any color that didn't belong, and prayed Sara had heard the shots and activated the radio signal. All he needed was for her to come dashing outside about now.

"Dammit," he muttered, "where are you, Roger? You had to hear those shots."

Levette was hysterical. He was literally frothing at the mouth, spittle foaming in tiny flecks and spewing from his lips as he cursed the man who'd fired the shots and cursed Mackenzie Hawk for not being dead.

"He knew! Even before you fired the shot, he knew. The bastard! That Indian spook knew. Do something! Do it now, I tell you! He won't get away from me again. Not this time."

Levette waved his gun in the air and then took aim at the cabin. Realizing he was too far away for a handgun to be effective, he pointed it instead at the hired thug who'd fired and missed. The man's face was a pasty white. He felt Levette's rage and fear like he'd never known flood his body. The boss didn't suffer mistakes and he'd just made two. His bowels roiled and he felt his bladder give way as a warm stream ran silently down his leg. It was the last thing he felt as Levette's bullet slammed into his head.

Hawk heard the shot in the woods off to his right and let in a small ray of hope. That had to be Roger and the Company men. They were going to come out any minute now, announcing everything was under control.

But no one came, and he waited, unable to get to Sara.

The tracker heard shots fired as they had planned and heard no answering gunfire. He rubbed his palms together in pleasure. *Good, good! It will be over soon and I can collect my money and get off this mountain.*

He'd also made a decision to get as far away from Levette as possible. Levette was on a course of self-destruct as far as the tracker was concerned and he wanted to be far away when he detonated. Emerging from his hiding place, he headed toward the front of the cabin.

It's almost too easy, Tracker thought, creeping up the steps and turning the doorknob on the front door. It was locked. He'd expected that. It was a simple matter soon solved with a small tool extracted from a leather case in his coat pocket. The tumblers in the lock turned over, giving him easy entry into the cabin. He slipped silently inside and stood quietly, absorbing sounds and scents, allowing his eyes to adjust to the darker room after the brightness of the outdoors. His gaze darted about; down a hallway to his left; the rooms off to the right, and finally his pale-blue gaze sharpened. He inhaled as he followed the path of the staircase with a look. *She is up there.*

His pulse quickened, anticipation sharpening his senses. He walked stealthily across the polished hardwood, leaving a trail of mud and dry grass.

Sara heard the front door open and fear gripped her heart and twisted it mercilessly within her chest. She heard the ominous silence a rescuer would not have observed and knew there was no more waiting. Hawk was either hurt or dead. He would have come for her if he could and Roger's men would have called out if it were them.

She looked wildly about the room, searching for some means of protection. The closet! Hawk's guns were there and they were loaded. *I can't miss if they get close enough, and if I do miss, I can still give them something to worry about.*

Sara crept on hands and knees into the depths of the closet and felt about for the hidden panel. It was easier the second time. She watched it spring back to reveal its deadly treasures. She grabbed a handgun, one of the less sophisticated ones, and hoped as she crept out of the closet, stationing herself in a corner facing the partially open door, that the blasted gun wasn't on safety. She didn't have time to figure that out. The stair creaked just the least bit. It was the second step from the top. It always creaked like that. Taking shaky aim at the door, Sara fought back the urge to scream.

"Sara," the voice beckoned from just outside the door. But she didn't answer. She had already accepted dying. She just wasn't going to make it easy for them when she did.

"Don't be afraid, Sara. I'm here to help you. I'll take you to your brother. He's waiting for you just outside the cabin."

You lie, she thought, and aimed toward the man's voice as her heart pounded loudly in her ears. She swallowed trying to eliminate the dryness in her mouth. Roger wouldn't send anyone. He'd come himself. Of that much Sara was certain.

The tracker knew she was there. He could smell her fear. Yet caution prompted him to step aside. He pushed the door the rest of the way open and a bullet took a piece of the door with it, barely missing his face. The shot echoed on the landing as he plastered himself flat against the wall.

Damn! The bitch isn't going to make this easy.

Anger made him careless. He fought down the emotion while plotting his next move. He suspected Sara wasn't very familiar with guns, but at this range, it hardly mattered. He decided to add a little confusion to the situation and fired three rapid shots into the room, aiming them at the ceiling. He wanted her alive, but . . . not at the cost of his hide.

Sara screamed as the shots hit and plaster and bits of sheetrock rained down on her head and face. She blinked rapidly, trying vainly to wipe the fragments from her eyes. She only saw the shadow of a man somersault into the room and come up standing with a gun pointed straight at her chest.

"Give me the gun, Sara," he ordered. But the smile on his face disappeared as he watched the woman's fear replaced with a mutinous expression he didn't think he liked.

"I don't think so," she whispered shakily, and watched his displeasure as she waved her gun in the general direction of his head and shoulders.

"Be careful," he yelled, and panic seized him. Her finger was tightening on the trigger. He could see the spasmodic reaction and pictured it all ending on a damn cold mountain in the hills of Oklahoma. He should have suspected this. Sara Beaudry wasn't the type to cry and beg. He'd known that. He'd made a mistake and Levette didn't suffer mistakes.

Sara backed toward the door, her gun still aimed, when the tracker made his move. Just as she reached the doorway and freedom, he jerked his gun upward, took aim at the right of her head and pulled the trigger. The carefully aimed shot sent splinters of the doorframe flying into her face and neck.

Sara turned, dropped her gun as she clasped her face in pain and terror and ran blindly down the stairs, blood pouring freely from her head and face.

"Just like in the movies," Tracker sneered, lunging after his prey.

He hit her from behind just as she gained the open door in the living room. Sara crumpled like a rag doll. The tracker grunted, pleased with his success. He bent over, lifted her onto his shoulders in a fireman's carry and went outside into the weak sunshine of Oklahoma winter with his bounty.

Hawk heard the shot inside the cabin and looked wildly about for help. Without further hesitation, he crawled from under the porch, ignoring the warning pressure from his injured ribs and scrambled up the porch steps, gun in hand. A rapid succession of shots made him drop to his stomach and he lay flat against the floor of the porch, only inches away from the back door and Sara.

A steady stream of curses fell from his lips as he railed Levette, the Company, and Fate. And then Sara screamed and the terror and pain he heard in her voice made him lose control. In a blinding rage, he grabbed the doorknob and fell into the backroom of the cabin with a hail of gunfire at his back. Impact on landing knocked the gun from his hand. Pain from his ribs shot throughout his body and momentarily paralyzed him. His mind blanked as he fought back a blackness that threatened his awareness.

"Damn," he moaned, "if they weren't broken before, they are now." He gingerly touched his burning chest and weakly kicked the back door shut before struggling weakly to his feet. The sounds of rapid footsteps running and stumbling down the stairs brought his attention sharply back into focus. It took but a few seconds to locate his gun and dash through the kitchen into the living room, but it was seconds too long. Hawk was just in time to see a man carrying Sara's limp body across the front yard toward the road that ran along the edge of the mountain.

He couldn't shoot. Sara's body was dangling limply down the man's back, preventing Hawk from a clear target. He shook with rage and terror as he watched his reason for living swiftly being carried beyond his grasp.

There was only one way left. He couldn't depend on the

Company for help. He'd done that before and shuddered, remembering where that had gotten him. Sara wasn't going to suffer the same fate as Marla.

Hawk was out the door and across the yard, swiftly following with no thought for his own safety. One single thought echoed over and over in his mind as his long legs diminished the distance between himself and Sara. If and when he survived this, he was going to take Colonel Harris apart and scatter him one piece at a time all the way down the Kiamichi. Hawk's eyes grazed the treeline as he hurried after the unsuspecting man carrying his Sara. *Where in hell is my backup?*

EIGHT

"We've got three, Captain Beaudry."

The hard-eyed young man with a week's worth of whiskers hunkered down beside his commander. He was part of the six-man team known throughout the Company as Beaudry's Bandits and proud of it. Although Beaudry was the only one in the team over thirty years old, there was not one among them who wasn't an expert at his job.

"Two in custody, one dead, sir. Not our work though. Looks like he displeased someone mighty highly."

The young man's drawl placed his origins from the Tennessee Valley. It was a story in itself how he'd come from Tennessee to D.C.; from a twenty-two caliber rifle and hunting squirrels to automatic weapons and hunting men.

Beaudry's thoughts were frantic as he tried to calm the panic rushing through his mind. "Has anyone seen Levette?" he asked, his words clipped and concise, just like Company policy.

"Sir, Martin reported a man with a rifle off to the north, close to the back of the cabin and another has entered the cabin."

"Dammit!" Roger muttered. "How did they break through our security? I thought we had that covered."

"Don't know for certain, Captain, but from the signs, one of them is awful good at trackin'. You know what I mean? Real clean entry, nothin' left behind. Wait, sir! There now . . . just comin' out of the house."

The young man's voice was calm and low as he watched a man exit the cabin with a woman's limp body slung over his shoulder. He raised his eyebrows, the only sign of surprise, as Roger Beaudry let loose a most impressive string of curses.

"That's Sara. The bastard has my sister. Can't get a clean shot from here. Might hit her."

"Sir! Report comin' in now."

The hand-held radio crackled softly as one of the Bandits reported from the other side of the clearing. "Tall, blonde male running out of the woods to your right, sir! Going the other way around the cabin toward the road."

Roger Beaudry barked a new set of orders to his squad before he signed off and turned to his young companion.

"Travis, you're the best marksman in the Company."

"Sir! Yes, sir," the young man nodded. It was why he was a Bandit. Not one man in the Company's force of thousands had a better eye.

"I need you to work your way around and fast. Try to get the man holding my sister. If he moves, if he puts her down, any movement that might . . ."

"Sir, I understand." The Tennessee Bandit would take no chances with an innocent woman's life at stake, but . . . he would also not miss if he took the shot.

Beaudry watched the clear eyes and confident manner of the young Bandit and knew he was probably the only chance Sara would have. It was obvious something had happened to Hawk, otherwise Levette's man wouldn't have her.

"Go, Travis . . . and good luck."

"Yes, sir! I'll do my best."

Roger knew no truer words were spoken as Travis slipped off through the trees. He moved at an angle toward Levette and the man carrying Sara as they met at the side of the road in front of the cabin.

Then Roger's heart skipped a beat. In spite of the chill mountain air, he started to sweat. Hawk! He was coming from the direction of the cabin, moving with no thought of concealment or caution. They were certain to spot him before he ever reached their position. And Roger could tell, even at this distance, Hawk had been injured.

Roger Beaudry started to move through the trees, barking new orders into his radio as he ran.

Levette chortled with glee as he saw the Indian fall through the back door of the cabin and lay sprawled on the floor, half in and half out of the room.

"I got him. I knew it, I knew it!" he yelled aloud, turning in a crazy circle, looking for someone to congratulate him. But there was no one to laugh and no one to answer him. He muttered an obscenity, dropped the empty rifle, and started around the cabin. He allowed himself a complacent smile as he saw Tracker with his prize. "Good, the fool has the girl. At least someone besides me did something right today."

Tracker was carrying the girl over his shoulder, letting her dangle roughly against his back as he walked. He saw Levette hurrying toward him and called aloud, "I've got her." He grinned, scrambling for a firmer grip on Sara's long, dangling legs.

Levette ran his hand down the length of Sara's body

and smiled in satisfaction. "You've done well. Come, hurry to the vehicle. Someone may have heard the shots and get nosey enough to investigate. Call in my men. I have what I came for."

Tracker nodded and gave the prearranged signal to Levette's men. He then turned and headed in the direction of their hidden truck, leaving Levette to follow behind. Tracker was beginning to feel the woman's weight as he walked toward the woods. He knew she wouldn't stay unconscious forever, but he had a needle full of stuff in the truck that would keep her out if he could just get there in time.

"The men are coming, sir," Tracker called over his shoulder to Levette as he heard the sounds of running footsteps and then for no reason other than instinct, he knew it was not Levette's men . . . and it was not over. It had been too easy. "Look out!" he shouted, as he clumsily tried to pivot about with Sara still in his arms. But he was not in time to stop Mackenzie Hawk.

Levette crumpled to the ground, hit behind the knees by Hawk's assault.

Roger knew he couldn't get close soon enough to help Hawk, there was too much ground between them. All he could do was run . . . and pray. His fears were confirmed as he saw Hawk tackle Levette.

The Tracker could feel awareness coming back into Sara's body. She wasn't hanging as limply as before. He turned his head sharply, searching the woods for Levette's men, but no one was in sight.

"What in hell?" he muttered, and started to drop the girl to go to Levette's assistance when instinct told him not to move. After all, the woman was his only shield and he was a careful man. So, he chose to stand and watch as Levette and the big Indian rolled over and over in the mud, each fighting desperately for the upper hand.

It seemed like a lifetime, but mere seconds had passed since Hawk had pulled Levette to the ground. The pain in his chest ballooned as he fought Levette and unconsciousness. He struggled, his hands locked about Levette's throat, pressing harder and harder into the straining muscles of Levette's neck.

Levette knew he was losing ground. His strength lay in the brilliant evil of his mind, not his strength of body and the Indian was too powerful. He felt the energy draining from his body as his brain became starved for oxygen. In one last feeble bid for freedom, he jabbed toward Hawk. And as he jabbed, his elbow accidentally connected with the injured portion of Hawk's midriff. Suddenly—miraculously—he was free.

Hawk's hands fell away from Levette as he clutched at his own chest, allowing Levette much needed time for respite. The stabbing pain in Hawk's chest sent the blinding light of day disappearing behind a wall of blackness. Eclipsed by Levette's blow, Hawk knew no more.

He didn't see the rage on Levette's face transformed to glee as he watched his nemesis, Mackenzie Hawk grow still. He didn't see Levette rise to his feet and take aim with a gun he pulled from his jacket. But he heard the shot as he fought back from the blackness to reality and slowly opened his eyes, blinking into focus past the white-hot pain that was trying to claim his sanity.

Everything seemed to be happening in slow motion. The shot rang out, Levette spun, staggering backwards from Hawk's prone body. Hawk saw Levette's surprise and heard him scream ''No'' as he clutched at his shoulder. With a look of stunned fury gouged into his face, Levette stepped off the side of the mountain into space and took the short way down.

The tracker saw the man aim and fire, heard Levette's body as it fell through the thickly wooded and brushy side of the mountain and knew fear. Beaudry! He wasn't supposed to be here. This whole fiasco was because of him and the information he supposedly had on Levette. What good was the girl going to do him if Beaudry had already reported to his superiors? What did this mean?

Damn Levette! he thought, *this was all for nothing.* His heart froze and he forgot to take a breath as he realized his predicament. First one thought and then another raced wildly about in his brain. What should he do? Drop her and run or take his chances with a federal kidnapping charge?

But Sara took the choice out of his hands as she began to struggle weakly in his arms. The tracker felt her sliding off his shoulder, taking his ticket to safety with her.

Roger! Thank God! Hawk thought and watched Levette disappear off the edge of the Kiamichi. This time the Company hadn't let him down. He saw his chance to free Sara from her attacker as she began to move. Blocking out the thought of the pain he knew was coming, he lunged forward in a crouching position and caught Sara just as she slid from the tracker's grasp. He had her safely in his arms before she ever hit the ground and gave the Tennessee Bandit the opportunity he needed to carry out his orders.

Roger watched with terrible satisfaction as Travis's shot found its mark and the tracker fell forward, facedown in the mud and snow.

"Captain Beaudry here," he growled into the radio. "Well done, Travis, well done! Call for a chopper. We've got some wounded." Then he paused, taking a deep breath and exhaling slowly before he continued. "It's all over boys, come on in."

Roger nudged Tracker's still form with his foot. A handful of chocolate candies rolled from a coat pocket into the mud.

"I'll be damned," he mumbled, "Tootsie Rolls." Then he shrugged and hurried to Sara and Hawk, unaware what an important part the little sweets had played in Tracker's downfall.

Sara felt herself falling and knew who caught her before she ever saw his face. A wild joy filled her heart.

"Hawk! Hawk! I thought you were dead." Sara buried her face into the side of his neck as she sobbed his name over and over.

But Hawk couldn't think past the panic as he felt the blood on Sara's face. "Baby—ssh, ssh," Hawk crooned, fighting to maintain consciousness, although his pain was increasing steadily. "It's all right, Sara. It's over . . . all over. But you need to let me look at you," he pleaded as he tried to pull her gently away. "Please, Sara, let me see what they did to you, baby."

Finally Sara acquiesced, relaxing her grip from around his neck and allowed him to lay her gently on the ground. She hiccupped and then moaned aloud as the spasm jarred her head. Shock was wearing off—with consciousness came the agony.

The side of her face burned like fire and she reached a shaky hand up to feel the damage. Her face felt sticky and swollen and she winced, moving her fingers carefully upon her face to the place at her hairline where the pain was the worst.

"Don't touch it, Sara," Hawk ordered as he gently pulled her hand away.

Her eyes collided with his and she shuddered as she

read his concern. Her chin quivered and she struggled with her words, trying to force back the panic she felt as she saw her blood-stained fingers. Movement to the side of her brought her brother Roger's face into focus and she read concern and fear in his eyes.

Roger's heart plummeted. The scratched and torn flesh on the side of Sara's face made him sick to his stomach. She had made her living with that face. Angry with himself for thinking in the past tense, he discarded the worry and let himself absorb the fact that she was alive. *Sara will heal,* he thought. *She has to.*

Roger reached down, ignored the blood congealing on her fingers and squeezed lightly to let her know he was there. "Honey, it's Roger. You are going to be okay. There's a chopper on its way right now. They'll have you fixed up in no time. It's only scratches and they'll heal. Shoot, you looked worse the time you fell from the pear tree into the blackberry vines underneath, remember?"

Sara smiled weakly and nodded. But she knew her face was bad. Roger was a terrible liar. Hawk wouldn't lie to her. She trusted him to tell her the truth, no matter how painful.

Sara turned her head as she started to speak to Hawk and the look on his face stopped her thoughts and nearly her heart.

Hawk opened his mouth wide and a groan escaped as he leaned back on his heels, trying to draw an easy breath. He squeezed his eyes shut against the clawing fingers of pain that constricted his heart and lungs. It was spreading. He could not blink without wanting to scream. He heard the helicopter clearing the crest of the Kiamichi and starting its descent, but it wasn't going to get here in time for him. Everything faded into shadows and then nothing. He fell back with Sara's name on his lips.

He didn't hear Sara's scream or Roger's frantic orders as the Bandits loaded him and Sara into the waiting helicopter. He didn't hear Beaudry issuing clean-up duty to the Bandits or order the pilot to Dallas Memorial. His world was dark, cold, and empty. Silent—but blessedly void of the pain.

The emergency room was a nightmare. Roger had flashed his badge as they unloaded Sara and Hawk from the helicopter and requested hospital security to stand by. If the media got wind of Sara Beaudry's return and the extent of her injuries, they'd have a field day. And if that wasn't enough grief for Roger, the doctors were balking at treating an unconscious man with no next of kin.

Roger shoved a beefy hand through his sandy hair and expelled an angry sigh. He thought the government had red tape! Never in his life had frustration threatened his civility as it did now. He was standing before a lady in emergency admitting, whom he desperately wanted to throttle.

"I'm sorry," she intoned nasally, and looked at him over her glasses. "That is hospital policy. Someone must sign for him . . . be responsible, you know."

"I said I'd sign," Roger growled, surpressing the urge to shout.

"No . . . you won't do. You've already stated you are not his employer, not related—sorry. You just won't do."

And then a familiar voice from behind Roger's bulky body spoke. Roger shrugged, stepped back out of the way and watched his baby sister straighten the kinks out of everyone and everything in sight.

Sara was a mess. Her head throbbed. Blood was caked and dried in the most unappealing places, but she could walk and she could talk and think . . . and all she was thinking about was Mackenzie Hawk.

"Excuse me," she said, her royal manner donned in spite of the lack of usual finery. "I want this man treated immediately. If you let him lie unattended another minute, I'll sue you and every employee of Dallas Memorial. Do I make myself clear?"

Even the orderly mopping floors down the hall stopped to listen.

"But, miss," the clerk stuttered, taken aback by Sara's appearance and manner, "the rule states . . ." She was reaching for a book lying on a shelf above the desk when Sara sent the whole shelf flying onto the floor.

"You want rules? I'll give you rules. Do you know who I am?"

The woman shook her head, certain that she was about to be told.

"My name is Sara Beaudry." And as luck would have it, one of her Wildcat commercials flashed on the screen of the portable TV sitting on the admitting desk. She pointed an accusing finger at the monitor. "That's me . . . and that's mine," she shouted, pointing at Hawk's still form. "And if you don't fix him, it's going to take a king's ransom to buy back your hospital's good reputation after I call a press conference."

Roger groaned and sank weakly against the wall of admitting. She'd done it now. He'd tried his best to keep a low profile and Sara had shouted it all over three floors.

"Well, of course, Miss Beaudry, we had no idea there was any family present."

The clerk glared accusingly at Roger, laying the blame for this unfortunate misunderstanding immediately at his feet. "Sign here, please."

And Sara Beaudry signed her name on the most important paper of her life.

Only after Sara was certain Hawk was receiving the best attention the hospital had to offer did she crumple, sobbing hopelessly on her brother's shoulder as she faced the tragedy of her own injuries. However, a stern-faced young doctor with soft eyes and gentle hands soon had the Texas Wildcat under control. Speaking in a low, calm voice, he methodically removed every splinter fragment from her face and neck as he reassured Sara of complete recovery. Sara watched a lab technician poke indelicately at a vein in her arm while wincing at the doctor's ministrations.

"Shoot, miss," he drawled, sponging disinfectant carefully on Sara's raw and burning face, "I've had worse scratches from fallin' off my horse."

"Do you know my brother?" Sara asked, turning a keen eye to await his answer. "You two tell remarkably similar stories."

But the doctor merely smiled and continued his work.

"Sara, please let me take you home," Roger pleaded, but to no avail.

Sara sat in stubborn silence in the darkened hospital room and tried to curl her legs into a comfortable position. Unfortunately for Sara's long legs, the chair wasn't made for comfort. But Sara wasn't budging. She wasn't leaving the hospital until Hawk went with her and he hadn't regained consciousness.

She held Hawk's hand and gently brushed across a bruise, watching his face for a sign of awakening.

"He's been hurt so many times, Roger." Sara's worried whisper made Roger frown. "This time we hurt him, next time . . . No, there won't be a next time if I have anything to say about it."

Roger stood and walked stiffly to the end of Hawk's bed, watching his ex-partner's too-still form with concern. He angrily shoved his hands into his pants pockets, making the fabric pull awkwardly across his bulky frame.

"No, Sara, we didn't hurt Hawk. Levette did."

Sara knew she hadn't been unconscious long this afternoon, but from the time Tracker stopped her flight from the cabin until she felt Hawk catch her in his arms, her world had very nearly come to an end. And her world consisted of this big man who lay much too still under the stiff, white linens on the hospital bed.

Sara rose from her chair and stretched, working the kinks from her stiff, bruised body. She grimaced as she carefully touched the bandaged side of her face. But she wasn't really concerned about her face any longer. She had seen before the bandages were applied that, except for the place in her hairlane, the scratches would heal with no scarring.

She was surprised at herself for the lack of concern she felt toward her injuries. Her face was a key part of her success and right now Sara couldn't even work up a small sweat about it. Every ounce of energy was being focused on this man who'd claimed her heart as he'd claimed his right to her body.

"Oh God, Roger, why doesn't he wake up?"

Roger knew his sister was nearly at her wit's end, but was at a loss to offer much comfort. Her happiness hinged solely on Hawk's recovery. And the doctors had been adamant in assuring them no vital organs had been damaged. But four broken ribs had placed a lot of pressure on his heart and lungs. He was just going to need time and rest. Unfortunately for Sara, patience was not one of her strong points of character.

Sara leaned over Hawk's bed, careful not to touch his

tightly bandaged chest and ribs, and brushed a tumbled lock of hair away from his face.

"He needs a haircut," she mumbled, resisting the urge to cry.

"Sara." Roger's low voice beckoned as she turned to face her brother's concern.

"What?"

"Do you love him?" Roger asked.

Sara didn't even hesitate nor had Roger expected her to do so. He already knew her answer before she uttered a word.

"Love? Such a small word for such a big feeling."

Tears pooled and overflowed as she turned back to Hawk and looked at him, watching his chest rise and fall under the carefully folded bed linens tucked around him. "Yes, I guess you could say I love him . . . if love means a reason for living until tomorrow; or the reason I draw my next breath. He's the other half of me, Roger. I can't face the thought of life without him."

Roger was at her side in an instant as he enfolded her in a loving embrace. Ever careful of her injuries, he tried to comfort her with his usual clumsy affection.

Hawk heard her voice before he ever focused on her words, and then when he did, he wanted to cry. Remaining still until he fully trusted himself to open his eyes and speak, he startled them both when he growled.

"You better be Roger Beaudry or you're in a hell of a lot of trouble, mister." It was hard to enunciate his words, but he knew he got his message across when the startled pair stepped quickly apart and stared at him in shock.

Sara's shock quickly turned into the beginnings of a smile before a grimace of pain pulled at her face instead.

"Good to hear a familiar threat," Roger quipped, masking his relief behind the teasing words as Hawk rewarded him with a sardonic grin.

"Sweetheart! You're awake! Thank God! Do you hurt? I'll call a nurse. I'll . . ."

"Sara, shut up and come here," Hawk whispered, weakly patting the side of his bed. As she obeyed, Hawk reached up and gently touched the side of her face, a worried question in his eyes.

"It's fine, really," she assured him, then fussed with his sheet and pillow, anything for an excuse to touch him. "Just scratches. I promise. The doctor put all this gauze on my face just to make himself look good and believe me, it'll take more than gauze before I consider this hospital redeemed."

Hawk raised his eyebrows questioningly at her impassioned speech and grinned a crooked grin as he asked Roger, "Did I miss something?"

"Well," Roger drawled, stepping back to avoid Sara's surreptitious kick, "let's just say the hospital delayed your treatment a bit too long and our little Wildcat nearly scratched their eyes out."

"Sara . . . baby . . . did you have another fit?" Hawk wanted to laugh, but he controlled the urge. It would hurt too much to give in to mirth.

"Somebody had to take care of you," Sara announced, "so I simply volunteered for the job. I told them you belonged to me and to put you back together ASAP."

Hawk's eyes glistened and the smile on his face disappeared as he whispered past a big lump in his throat, "You told them I belonged to you, huh?"

"Yes," she answered, and dared him to argue. She had just had about enough of his hesitancy and reluctance to trust her because of some other woman's stupidity and greed. The look on his face made her heart pound and her stomach did a nosedive toward the soles of her shoes. *Darn you, Mackenzie Hawk*, Sara worried, *you better not pull back in your shell again.*

"Did you happen to mention that it works both ways, baby?"

Please God, make him mean what I think he means! and she shook her head no.

"Well, you better find someone quick and tell them because if you don't, I will. The next time I wake up and my woman is hugging another man . . ."

Hawk never got to finish his speech. Sara was in his arms.

Roger decided now was as good a time as any to make an exit. He needed to check on his men and get the details to complete his final report. All in all, it had been one hell of a Christmas Eve, but from the look of things it was going to be a great Christmas.

NINE

Sara put the finishing touches on her makeup, a tricky business around a face still sporting several butterfly bandages. She stepped back from the mirror for a full view of her handiwork and smiled to herself, imagining Hawk's reaction to her outfit. He hadn't seen her wear anything but jeans and this outfit was going to be quite a change.

It was an old modeling trick Sara incorporated to call attention away from a physical fault by accentuating an asset. No one was going to notice her face when they got a good look at her hair . . . and her dress.

The phone rang, breaking her train of thought and Sara rolled her eyes in frustration and called out to her brother.

"Roger, would you get that, please? I refuse to talk to any more reporters. I want to hurry and get to the hospital.

Hawk was being released today and she didn't want to keep him waiting. Sara had spent Christmas Day and most of the day after that in the hospital at Hawk's bedside. Finally, at Roger's and Hawk's insistence, she'd come home. It had been great to sleep in comfort in her own bed, but not great to sleep alone. It hadn't taken Hawk long to become a necessity in Sara's life. That was why she was in a hurry to get to Dallas Memorial. She wanted Mackenzie Hawk. She wanted him home with her. And she wanted it now.

She bounced into the living room and twirled around, billowing the flared skirt of her minidress.

"How do I look?" she asked, waiting for her brother's nod of approval.

Roger frowned, speaking into the phone in low, measured tones and it was with great difficulty he forced a smile and a thumbs up sign for Sara's benefit.

Sara was in such a state of excitement, she missed the worried expression on Roger's face as he disconnected. She took a final look in the mirror and decided she would do. The fiery cloud of hair that floated about her face and down her back and the russet colored China-silk dress that was clinging to every hollow and curve of her body would do all right. What exactly it would do remained to be seen. Roger watched his sister's excitement with mixed emotions. The outfit she was wearing certainly accomplished . . . things. Texas men being what they were, Roger hoped Sara wouldn't start a riot.

"Oh, I almost forgot," she called as she dashed back to her bedroom, returning with a large shopping bag in one hand and her soft, cream-colored cashmere coat in the other.

"Come on, Roger," she chided, as if she'd been waiting for him for hours and not the other way around. "You're going to have to run interference for me. There's an absolute mob in the parking lot. If I'd known years ago that an unscheduled disappearance would get this much publicity, I might have tried it sooner."

She grinned as he put on his cop face and ushered her out the door.

Roger bulldozed her past well-wishers, plopped her into the passenger seat of her car with little ceremony, and peeled out of the condominium complex, leaving Wildcat tracks on the Dallas streets.

Sara raised her eyebrows, but wisely refrained from making remarks about his driving.

"I've always wanted to do that," he grinned, forcing himself to play along with Sara's gaiety. She'd been through so much. It was great to see her smiling again. He couldn't have been happier about the growing relationship between Sara and Hawk. Roger was well aware of the kind of man his sister was getting, he just prayed she was going to get to keep him.

"Miss Beaudry, Miss Beaudry!" a newsman shouted, rudely shoving a microphone in her face. "Could we have some comment from you about your mysterious disappearance? There have been rumors about a kidnapping attempt. Is there any truth to the story? Is the man with you a bodyguard?"

Sara turned her professional face to the mini-cam aimed in her direction and smiled. She'd already been coached by Roger as to just how much she could and could not say.

"I have had an accident as you can obviously see, but I assure you, the injuries are merely scratches and," she linked arms with Roger and patted his shoulder, "this isn't my bodyguard, at least no more than any brother would be."

"Brother? But, Miss Beaudry . . . what about the reports that state you've been visiting a certain man regularly here at Dallas Memorial and he's definitcly not your brother? What do you have to say to that? Was there someone with you when you had your accident?"

Sara sighed, but kept the smile pasted on her face. She would like to tell them all what to do with their reports, but it would have to be censored first. And as her manager, Morty, was fond of reminding her, "It's not good for business to antagonize the press."

"Please," Sara begged, "I've said all I intend to say at this time, but if you'll let me enter, you can ask the man himself when we return, okay?"

Sara left on that cryptic comment as Roger pulled her into the hospital, shoving his way past the shouts, microphones, and cameras.

"They're going to have a field day with that remark, honey," he chided.

"Hawk can take care of them," she said. "They'll have the shortest, most succinct interview they've ever encountered when they shove a microphone in Mackenzie Hawk's face. They'll be lucky if he doesn't put it somewhere they find extremely painful." She laughed aloud at the thought and then grimaced as the laugh pulled painfully at her healing face.

Sara's pulse quickened and she quelled the impulse to run as she and Roger exited the elevator. As she drew closer to the nurse's station, she realized she'd probably delayed just a bit too long in arriving. It looked like Hawk had been waiting for her and none too patiently if she was to believe the commotion and flurry at the station.

"Miss Beaudry, thank goodness you've arrived!"

A fresh-faced young candy striper carrying an armload of magazines scurried from Hawk's room. "He's been a bit . . . upset, and you seem to be the only one who can do much with him. If you know what I mean." Then she giggled and blushed at the wry expression on Sara's face.

"Miss Walker," the RN on duty scolded as she shooed the little volunteer along, "I'm certain you're not finished with your duties; run along please."

Then she handed Sara a handful of papers and deftly maneuvered a wheelchair toward Hawk's room without waiting for either of them. "We've been waiting for you." She smiled sardonically and raised an eyebrow. "It seems Mr. Hawk has no clothes to put on and he absolutely refuses to leave his room without them."

"Oh Lord!" Sara said apologetically, "I intended to get here sooner. There were just so many people downstairs it took longer to get through than I had anticipated. I'm sorry about the delay."

"Don't apologize to me. I'm not the one in a snit." She grinned, parked the wheelchair outside Hawk's room, and said as she walked away, "Call me when you're ready to leave. Those are his discharge papers. I'll wheel you down to the lobby when you've coaxed him into . . . a better mood."

"I'll just wait here," Roger muttered, and flopped into the wheelchair.

"Coward," Sara chided, and pushed open the door to Hawk's room.

Hawk stood at the window, his back to the door. He was wearing the bottom of a pair of hospital pajamas, a lot of bandages, and nothing else. He heard the door open and growled without ever turning around. "No more tests! No more needles! No more damn baths! Do I make myself perfectly clear?"

"Perfectly, darling," Sara crooned. She was rewarded by Hawk's look of pleasure as he pivoted about. Then his jaw slacked and his arms dropped loosely at his sides. He took a long, stunned look at the woman standing just inside his room. She looked like the "Wildcat that ate the canary." She was beautiful.

"Sara?" he said, suddenly unsure how to approach this walking dream.

"Did you miss me?" she asked, sauntering over to him.

Miss her? Hawk wondered. *I'm not sure I know this Sara. I think I miss the old one.*

Hawk couldn't take his eyes from her. *Who is this stranger?* he wondered.

Sara slid her arms around his neck and pressed her soft, cool lips against the jut of his chin.

Hawk pulled her closer, shut his eyes, and slowly ran his hands across the gentle swell of Sara's hips. The brown silk was as soft and smooth as the skin on her body and he smiled to himself as she leaned into him. This was the Sara he knew.

"Got a problem?" she asked, and tilted her head back just the least bit so Hawk could get the full effect of her new look.

"Yeah, I've got one. I'm just not sure this room is private enough to take care of it."

He bent down and nipped the side of her mouth. It opened to protest the harsh treatment and Hawk pounced, taking possession with a subtle thrust of his tongue. Sara moaned, accepting his domination with pleasure and leaned into Hawk, running her hands up his back where she accidentally encountered the layers and layers of bandages.

"Oh!" she gasped, pulling away from his kiss. "I forgot. Am I hurting you, sweetheart?" Her hands lightly grazed the layers of gauze and her eyes grew round as she waited anxiously for his assurances. The last thing Sara wanted to do was hurt him again.

"Yeah, I'm hurting. Can you feel it?" he whispered, and rubbed his lower body against her stomach.

She felt the thrust of his body and an answering need blossomed deeply within her.

"That's real cute, Indian," she sighed and carefully nestled against his chest.

Hawk grinned to himself and nuzzled the hair at her neck, while cherishing the woman in his arms. "Lady, you smell great, look fantastic, and . . ." then a frown dug into his forehead and a familiar, formidable expression appeared.

What now? Sara wondered.

"What do you have on underneath this thing?" His voice rumbled like thunder in the distance.

"More than you do, mister."

Hawk sank against the window sill and held up his hands in defeat. "I forgot. When it comes to arguments, you win. I give . . . okay?"

"Sure, as long as you remember that tonight."

Sara clung suggestively to him and gave him a tongue-in-cheek, ultra-sexy look. Then, his lack of clothing reminded her of the very reason for her trip to the hospital, and she grabbed the shopping bag she'd brought from the apartment.

"Roger did a little shopping for you yesterday. Some of your things were pretty far gone. They were so bloody . . . and torn."

Her voice became a whisper as she clutched the bag to her chest, remembering the horror they'd been through.

"Don't, Sara. It's over. And I'm going to spend the rest of my life making certain nothing like that ever happens to you again. I promise."

Hawk coaxed a smile to her face and the clothes from

her arms. He'd had all of a hospital he could stand. As soon as he dressed, he ushered Sara from the room.

Roger was evicted from the wheelchair and Hawk surprised them all by sitting meekly while being wheeled to the lobby. He'd do whatever it took to leave. Unfortunately, he hadn't counted on the mob awaiting his exit. Sara's cryptic remark had them all waiting for a glimpse of the man who'd tamed their Texas Wildcat.

"Hell," he muttered, looking at the mob plastered to the glass doors in the lobby and rose with purpose from the wheelchair. He glared accusingly at Sara's suspiciously angelic expression.

"Here's where they separate the men from the boys," Roger said. He ignored Sara's glare as she thrust their belongings in his outstretched arms.

"Morty sent a limo, Roger. Hawk can't squeeze his hurt self into that little bitty sportscar. You take it home for me, okay?"

Sara grinned at the pleased expression on her brother's face. He liked her car a bit too much.

The tight bandages cautioned Hawk not to hurry and he suppressed the urge to grab Sara and run.

"Come on, lady. Let's get this over with. What have you been telling these vultures, anyway?" Hawk mumbled, as he took Sara by the arm and opened the door only to be greeted by chaos.

For several seconds the emerging trio was blinded by the flash of camera lights. People shouted so many questions at once, it was all Hawk could do to keep Sara and himself from being crushed in the melee. Sara was unusually silent and Hawk suspected he was being put to some kind of test.

It took a minute or two for the reporters to realize that the man hadn't said a word in answer to any of them.

Instead, he stood between the throng and Sara Beaudry with an enigmatic expression on his face.

Sara recognized it and allowed herself a tiny bit of relief. That was his stubborn face. He was going to do just fine.

One pushy reporter shoved a microphone through the crowd directly under Hawk's nose. Hawk turned and fixed the man with a cold, green stare and then drawled,

"Is that thing edible?"

"What? Oh . . . oh, I uh . . ." the reporter stammered, surprised by the absurdity of the question.

"Well then," Hawk ordered, "get it out of my face."

With that pungent remark prefacing her introduction, Sara slipped an arm under his elbow for moral support and announced,

"Ladies and gentlemen, Mackenzie Hawk. I owe him my life, but he only wanted my heart . . . so I gave it to him."

Snickers and giggles erupted from the crowd as Hawk flashed a smile at Sara that left no one wondering how this big man had snared the most sought after lady in Texas. He was dynamite himself. Pens scratched first impressions on paper as the crowd settled back and began asking questions in an orderly manner.

"Mr. Hawk, what is your relationship to Miss Beaudry?"

"None . . . yet," he answered with a slight smile curving the sexy cut of his lips. "He's the only relative here." Hawk pointed toward Roger Beaudry who was leaning against a wall, watching the crowd with his cop face in place.

"Well then, let me phrase my question a bit differently. Are you the new man in Sara Beaudry's life?"

Sara held her breath; her face giving away none of her

apprehension while awaiting his answer as anxiously as the media.

"No, I'm not the new man. I'm the only man."

Cheers and scattered applause followed his remark and he felt Sara squeeze his elbow. Hawk pressed her arm to his side in an understanding gesture as he fielded the media like a pro.

Sara was seeing a new side to this enigmatic man she loved so desperately, and she liked what she saw. *I'm going to have to drag him off that mountain more often. I wonder what else he's hiding from me?*

She could tell Hawk was out of patience and beginning to tire. She quickly scanned the crowd for the car her manager had promised. Morty waved from his place by the limousine to get Sara's attention and intercepted her signal that they were ready to leave.

"Mr. Hawk, please. Just one more question," the obstinate reporter shouted, rudely pushing the microphone back into Hawk's face.

Hawk sighed and winced at the pain that squeezed his chest.

"What?" came his terse reply.

"What does the future hold for you and Miss Beaudry? Are there wedding bells in the distance, or do you plan to cohabitate without a license?"

Hawk's eyes grew cold and his smile flattened as the man's rudeness angered him and shocked the crowd. But he maintained a calm demeanor and ended the questions with his next remark.

"I'll bet you're the kind of guy who reads the last chapter of a book before he buys it, and then has no surprise waiting for him at the end. Quite frankly, it's none of your damn business."

The crowd cheered and parted amiably to let Sara and

Hawk pass as Morty stood by the car, waiting for his meal ticket to appear.

"Jesus!" Hawk groaned, sinking back against the upholstered luxury in the limousine and stretched his long length into a more comfortable position.

"You were wonderful, Hawk, and I'm very sorry for all this," Sara gestured to the dispersing crowd of journalists. "All this is a part of my life. I wasn't sure you would keep me if I warned you ahead of time what was in store."

Sara's anxious expression clouded her usually shining eyes.

Hawk frowned and pulled her carefully against him, barely acknowledging Morty's presence in the limo as it pulled into traffic.

"Not keep you, little Wildcat?" he whispered, and planted a kiss on her worried mouth. "I don't have a choice. You're my world, Sara. Don't you know that yet?" He pulled her head back onto his shoulder and held her dearly against his heart.

Sara heard the reverence in his voice and felt the steady beat of his heart against her ear and smiled to herself.

Morty, however, sat in nervous silence and watched Sara Beaudry slipping farther and farther from his grasp.

"Morty, thanks for arranging all this," Sara said. "I hope you've cancelled all my pressing contractual agreements as I asked. I'm certain none of the sponsors wish to use damaged goods, anyway," she muttered, lightly touching the injured side of her face.

Hawk looked at Sara, guilt and concern for her and her career uppermost in his mind, but remained silent as they neared their destination.

"Sure, sure, sweetheart," Morty said. "But you don't need to worry about yourself. You're still in hot demand, baby. This all just added icing to the cake. Everyone will

want to see for themselves that you're still good as new
. . . and you soon will be. Trust me, baby. Trust me."
He familiarly stroked Sara's leg as he had done so often
in the past, only to withdraw his fingers in panic, looking
frantically to see if they were all still in place.

The look that Indian had given him when he touched
Sara had nearly stopped his heart. *Damn him anyway!*
Morty thought with stunned finality as the ramifications of
Mackenzie Hawk's presence in Sara Beaudry's life finally
hit home. His devious mind started turning over the mea-
gre possibilities for replacing Sara Beaudry. But he had
no clients that even came close to her quality and he knew
as they reached her apartment and watched her walk away,
that Sara Beaudry was irreplaceable.

She was one-of-a-kind.

Sara's apartment was just as Hawk imagined. Like Sara,
it was all open spaces with a comfortable air of welcome.
Earth tones dominated the color scheme and were accented
by vivid splashes of bright blue and verdant green. Big
overstuffed furniture made for comfort and long legs rested
on a deep pile carpet that beckoned bare feet to linger and
enjoy.

Hawk leaned his head against the cushioned back of the
sofa and closed his eyes. He couldn't place the feeling
that kept welling inside of him, or the emotions and sensations it evoked. At times it threatened to overwhelm him,
and other times it filled him so completely, he felt no
room left for breath. But the peace that came with it was
immeasurable for a man such as Hawk. A solitary, often
lonely man, who no longer craved isolation; all he craved
now was Sara. He had known for some time that he could
resurrect this tremendous feeling simply by saying Sara's
name or picturing her face; remembering the way she felt

beneath him as he drove his aching body deeply within her womanly warmth. She completed him.

Hawk felt the sofa give as Sara sat down beside him. She was being careful not to bump anything bandaged on either of them. Hawk felt her hand touch gently on his pant leg and his thigh muscles tightened as Sara stroked the inner side of his leg. A familiar ache began to tighten in his lap as well and he had to stop her before she drove all his good intentions out of his mind.

He captured her hand just as it journeyed into dangerous territory and held it hostage against his thigh. He opened his eyes, capturing her attention with a look. She was so willful and beautiful, so gallant and hurt. And so much in love with him he felt it flowing from her body to his by the mere touch of her hand. His voice shook as he pulled her hand to his lips and reverently kissed each delicate fingertip before he spoke.

"I let them get to you, Sara. I let them hurt you and for that, I'll never forgive myself."

He stopped her coming argument with a touch of his finger to her lips and turned her around, using his lap as a pillow for her head. Her hair cascaded down his legs as she allowed Hawk whatever liberty he desired. Hawk buried his hands in the willful abandon of her hair and then he touched the side of her face, a butterfly soft touch he could not resist.

Sara saw his eyes brimming in a sea of green regret as remorse for her pain and suffering overwhelmed him.

"Don't, Hawk," she begged. "It will heal, darling, just as you will heal."

She removed his hand from her injured face and placed it over her heart, holding it against the softness of her breast.

As he caressed the generous curves, he slipped his hand

inside the loose neckline of her dress, laying his fingers directly against her heartbeat. He felt the quickening beneath his sensitive touch and marveled that such a beautiful body could contain an even more beautiful soul.

"Sara."

His voice beckoned as it promised and Sara turned her head to see him better. She felt his other hand tighten its hold in her hair and sensed his extreme agitation.

"Do you know you are my life, little Wildcat? Before you, I was alive, but I didn't live. I saw smiles, but didn't hear laughter. Before you, I was a man, but now you make me a king." He took a deep breath, willing himself to continue before he lost his nerve. "Will you love me, Sara . . . and let me love you more until I die? Will you be my love . . . and my wife?"

Hawk waited, his mind refusing to accept what his heart already knew. Sara was already his.

Dear God! Sara thought, watching his anxious face. *Doesn't he already know the answer?*

Here again was the man who slept on satin sheets. The gentle sensuous lover who held her all through the darkness and into the dawn.

"My Hawk," Sara whispered through her tears. "Do you hear me say that? I've already told Texas and half the free world. Why are you the last to hear me?" She chided the fear and uncertainty from his eyes and replaced them with joy. "I'm already yours. Your love, your whatever you choose. Be it on your head if you want me as a wife."

Their laughter and joy echoed throughout her apartment as Mackenzie Hawk circled the earth no more. He had finally found his way home. However, neither of them realized that he would not be allowed to stay.

TEN

There was pain—so much pain. Sometimes he couldn't remember who he was or why he couldn't find his way out of these trees and back to the real world where he belonged. And then there was the cold, teeth-jarring, bone-aching cold that never went away. Sometimes, if he curled up just right and pulled enough damp, rotting leaves over him, a sort of steam would form between his body and the leaf cover and for a few blessed hours he would feel some sort of comfort. But it never lasted. Either he turned wrong in uneasy slumber, putting too much body weight on parts of his body that were injured, and they were many, or something in the dark—unseen and fearsome—moved too close to him and he would come awake. Then he would sit, hunched in a small, agonized mass of humanity and moan, a low, mournful cry not unlike that of the wolves he heard nightly in the distance.

There was also hunger. Nothing he had ever experienced before had prepared him for the deprivation he now endured. Only once had he seen anything resembling food.

161

The rest of the time, whatever he swallowed that didn't come back up counted as food.

He'd stumbled onto a bush with bright red clusters of hard little berries hanging a tantalizing distance above his reach. Levette spent the entire day struggling with a long, broken branch, trying in vain with his one good arm to knock down some of the berries. Fortunately for him, although he was not to know, his inability to reach the fruits saved his life. They were deadly poison. His anticipation had dwindled to frustration and frustration had boiled into debilitating anger and fury at the food he imagined just out of his reach. It was the coming nightfall on the mountain that had halted his futile harvest. He shuffled away to his hiding place, letting his injured arm dangle bloody and useless at his side while he cursed the fates and Mackenzie Hawk.

Levette remembered being shot and the fall down the mountain. It was just becoming harder and harder to remember why it had all happened. There had been too many days and nights of feverish hunger. It had driven away the need to remember anything except trying to survive. Therein lay Levette's prime problem. He didn't know how to survive on the Kiamichi. There was fresh water less than an hour's walk from him, but his fear of venturing too far from familiar territory kept him from ever finding it. He knew there was food in the cabin above him, but his injuries prevented climbing and so he endured. Injured, suffering from exposure and the beginning of starvation, Levette succumbed to an animal's survival instincts when hurt. He hid.

In the beginning when he had closed his eyes to rest, a man's face—a dark man with long, black hair and wild, green eyes—would flash into his consciousness and he would know ungovernable fury. But as the days passed, the emotions and the memory began to fade and now nothing entered his mind when he closed his eyes but a black hole that kept opening, opening. He sensed that one day he would not return from the darkness that claimed him as he slept.

He began to move about at night and stay hidden during the day after he started hearing the voices. At first he'd imagined they belonged to his men who'd come to rescue him and then he would remember. His men were dead, captured. These voices belonged to the men who'd hurt him. He had to stay hidden or they'd find him and hurt him again. He heard them moving about in the thick trees and brush below, but he felt safe in the old wolf den he'd claimed for his own. It was just that it was so small he kept bumping himself and reinjuring old wounds as he tossed about. It was then that the pain would rocket to the top of his head and tiny shrieks of agony slipped past his tightly pressed lips in spite of his desire to remain undetected.

If he wasn't hurt, he could get away. He would go back to . . . he would . . . nothing came to mind anymore and he was unable to finish the thought. He knew he was coming closer and closer to that black hole in his mind and one day he would fall completely through it.

He was so hungry. When it got dark, he would go out again. Maybe this time he'd find something besides the damp leaves he sucked on for moisture. This time he would not chew them in a fit of hungry desperation and try to swallow them to appease the knife-sharp claws of hunger that had nearly shredded their way through his belly. He had never managed to swallow the leaves anyway. He would always begin to hack and cough, choking as he vomited up the dusty shards along with tiny spittles of blood. Then the pain would surface and the hell would start all over again.

Several times of late, he had begun to envision dying. He was to the point of welcoming the idea. But as fate . . . or justice would have it, Levette couldn't even die to gain peace. Instead, he lingered and with each passing day became less and less of the human race and more and more of the animals that existed on the Kiamichi Mountain.

Twice in the moonlit darkness on the mountain, he'd sensed he was being followed. He was alerted by the short woofs of breath and low gutteral growls as they moved on four legs through the leaf-covered floor of the forest. The wolves knew this human was hurt, but for some reason they did not attack or even come closer. Levette stood, bracing himself against the back of a tree, a short club of a stick in his hand and waited. Panic increased his heartbeat until he could barely ascertain his short, jerky breaths from the circling pack and their quiet growls of warning. In terror and an odd desire to let come what may, he threw the stick into the darkness and heard it connect with a thud as a sharp yelp of pain echoed into the night sounds of the Kiamichi. The wolves hadn't come back again until last night. Then they had circled him before he was even aware they were present. But this time, unknown to Levette, the wolves had sensed something about him that was different. He had become less of a human and more of the animal world of the mountain. His odd, eratic behavior seemed to frighten them away rather than incite them. However, Levette knew none of this and had curled himself into a ball, awaiting their charge, preparing himself, almost welcoming the tearing of flesh that would bring an end to his suffering. But it never came, and he fell asleep on the floor of the forest.

A crow's sharp, stringent caw and the scolding a red

squirrel was giving the blue jay in the tree above his head awoke him with a start. Early signs of dawn had already emerged through the skeletal tree branches and Levette literally crawled in panic back to his den before the sun's brightness could reveal him to his enemies.

He shuddered with renewed fear as he pulled the branches back in place at the front of his hole in the mountain. He'd almost been caught. A tiny trickle of warmth ran down the inside of his leg and he looked down in surprise to see if he'd injured himself some more in his haste to seek shelter. But it wasn't blood he smelled, it was urine.

It was then Levette felt the black hole open fully in his mind and the fear began to pull him in. He'd been so afraid of the sunlight, he'd wet his pants. He curled himself up as best he could in the little hell-hole he'd been sleeping in and began to smile. It was no longer a beautiful smile. All the surface beauty was gone from this man. And then the chuckle, evil in its very intensity erupted from his throat like the bile that came up with the leaves he'd tried to eat. The chuckle became a laugh, gut-wrenching sobs mixed with maniacal hysterics until it finally pushed him over the edge. When he finally silenced, he looked about with a puzzled expression and then sniffed the air. Secure in the sense that he was safe and undetected, he kicked aside the wetness beneath him and curled into a crumpled ball.

Levette had finally escaped. All that remained was the shell that had housed unimaginable evil.

It turned over once during the early morning hours when sounds from far below indicated they were back—looking, looking, always looking. Cracked and bloodied lips curled back over teeth that were once pristine white and drew into a snarl as It heard the voices coming closer. But

It didn't move, and the dark, fathomless eyes remained motionless, staring with intensity toward the cave entrance. Soon the sounds receded. It growled softly in satisfaction and once again all was quiet on the Kiamichi.

Sara was furious with her brother. She hadn't seen him since day before yesterday at the hospital. He had called once, but used the excuse that he wanted to give them time alone. Sara knew what he wanted. He didn't want to bring her car back and she had a doctor's appointment in less than an hour. This was the day the last of the stitches came out of her head. Entirely too much had been made of the fact that her face had been scratched. She hadn't been disfigured or even scarred. Hawk had been hurt much worse than she, but everyone made the fuss over her recovery. Granted, she made her living with her body and looks, but there was more to her than surface and Sara's indignation flamed as she threw clothes about the bedroom while trying to decide what to wear to the appointment.

Hawk walked through the doorway just as a green, leather boot came flying through the air. He caught it just before it connected with a part of his anatomy he'd just as soon not have injured, and grinned at the look of shock on Sara's face and the other tell-tale boot dangling limply from her hand.

She let it drop to the floor and walked toward Hawk with her hands outstretched, a look of apology uppermost on her face.

"Have mercy, baby," Hawk begged with a chuckle, as he gathered the repentant redhead into his embrace.

"I'm sorry," Sara muttered into the front of Hawk's shirt and slipped her arms carefully around his chest, conscious of the tight bandages still binding his ribs. "It's not you I'm mad at, it's my darn brother. He still has my car and now we'll have to take a cab to the doctor's office unless I call Morty.''

Sara knew before he spoke what Hawk's answer would be to that suggestion. He and Morty had struck more sparks off each other than a summer storm.

''We'll call a cab,'' he growled and grabbed a handful of hair, pulling gently at it until he made Sara take her face from the front of his shirt and face him.

''That's what I thought you'd say,'' Sara grinned. ''I've already called for one. It's due in less than ten minutes and I'm not dressed.''

''That's a signal for my exit, little Wildcat, because when I get you alone in a bedroom, I don't put clothes on you, I take them off . . . remember?''

The smirking grin on his face and the dancing lights in his eyes made her heart turn completely over before it came to rest with a thud. She knew that look. She'd even prayed for it. She'd put it there, and now that it was more or less a permanent fixture in Hawk's eyes, she had to learn how to cope with the weak-kneed feeling she developed each time it appeared.

Playfully, Sara pushed Hawk out of her bedroom and grabbed the first outfit she touched in her closet. It didn't matter what she wore, clothes were clothes and she had places to go and people to see before indulging herself with that man.

Sara snorted at her reflection in the mirror as she gave a final check to her appearance before leaving. Here she was, counting the duties and chores that must be completed before she and Hawk could be alone together. *I need help*, she thought.

She saw him waiting for her across the room and sighed at the picture he presented. Somewhere between untamed and barely housebroken just about covered it, she decided and then watched him come toward her with purpose in each step. *Nope*, she decided, as he wrapped her in her coat and his arms, *It's too late for help*.

"I'm crazy, crazy in love with Mackenzie Hawk," Sara said against his mouth as she stole a quick kiss in the elevator on the way down to the lobby of her apartment complex. She relished the territorial look it put on his face as she pulled away.

"My God, woman!" Hawk muttered, as the elevator doors opened with a slap and thud. "You pick the damnedest times to start something."

Sara smiled to herself and shuddered with a quick shiver of anticipation. Hawk would make her pay for that later tonight. She could hardly wait.

ELEVEN

Sara left Hawk fidgeting beneath the receptionist's adoring gaze as she entered the examining room ahead of the specialist.

He was reputed to be one of the best plastic surgeons in Dallas, according to Morty, and had been assigned to oversee the emergency room handiwork on her face.

"Just a couple more stitches to come out and we'll be finished, Miss Beaudry," the doctor said in his best assuring manner. "That fellow in E.R. did a fine job on you. I couldn't have done a better job myself. I think he missed his calling. He's got a real light touch with a needle. That's what it takes to be good at this stuff."

Sara blinked in agreement, trying not to move as he slowly removed the tiny stitches. She let his voice flow over her without actually concentrating on his words, until he repeated his last question with some vehemence.

"I'm sorry, what did you say?" Sara asked and flashed him one of her best professional smiles as an apology.

It took the doctor a moment to remember what he'd

been saying and he stuttered a bit before repeating his question.

"I asked if you had needed all of the pain pills they gave you?"

"No, I don't think I took more than one or two. I don't even know for sure where they are. I don't take much medicine," and then she winced as he pulled out the next to last stitch.

"Sorry," he mumbled, as he peered closely in her hairline for the last tiny stitch. "That's good," he continued. "It's fortunate that the doctor in E.R. did a thorough workup on you when you were admitted. It could have been unfortunate to prescribe something that might have harmed the baby. Pregnancy is a tricky thing to deal with in emergency. Now, take a deep breath, this is the last stitch and it may sting a bit."

Sara took a deep breath all right, but not because he told her to. It was the word baby, followed by pregnant that stopped her heart. And it wasn't pain from the stitch that spilled tears out and over her cheeks to slide silently down her face. It was joy.

Dear, sweet Lord, she was going to have his child. Nothing on earth could have prepared her for the flood of pure peace and contentment that filled her. Of course, she was pregnant. They had done nothing to prevent it. The only thing their lives had focused on was living through the next day.

"Are you okay?" the doctor asked as he anxiously dabbed at her head. He hadn't expected this kind of reaction. She'd seemed made of sturdier stuff. Then something occurred to him. Surely she'd known about the pregnancy, although she wasn't very far along. Women were supposed to know about such as this even before doctor's fancy tests.

"You did know about the pregnancy, didn't you?" he asked.

Sara opened her eyes and smiled.

"Hmmmh? What? Oh yes, certainly I knew," she whispered, and then threw her arms around his neck and planted a kiss on his pudgy cheek. "And I'm more than okay. I'm fantastic."

She sure is, the doctor thought as he watched her leave his examining room.

Hawk looked up, startled at the way Sara dashed into the waiting room. He took one look at her tear-stained face and couldn't reconcile it with the smile she was wearing.

"You've been crying," he growled, as he pulled her into his arms, oblivious to any bystanders.

"It was nothing," she whispered, kissing him quickly beside his earlobe as she pulled him out the door. "Just good news. I always cry when I'm happy."

Hawk looked long and hard at Sara's blooming countenance and decided she was telling the truth. He pushed aside her hair for a closer inspection as they waited outside for a cab. He breathed a long, long sigh of relief at the tiny scars he knew would soon disappear.

"I'm fine," Sara scolded and pulled his hand away from her head to her lips, kissing the palm before she placed it against his heart.

"From me to you," she said, and then felt her feet leave the ground as Hawk whirled her around before pulling her into a fierce bear hug.

"Lady, you're going to have to stop doing this stuff in public. I've been out of polite company so long I just might forget where we are and embarrass the hell out of both of us. You hear me?"

His words were threatening, but his touch was not as

he walked off the curb with deadly purpose and almost dared the next empty cab to run over him.

"Need a ride, buddy?" the cabby drawled, as he reluctantly took the fare. He'd been off-duty and on his way home. This guy just didn't look the kind to refuse.

Sara felt herself propelled inside, quickly muttered the address to the cab driver, and then closed her eyes. Hawk was in no condition to talk as he swooped downward. Sara felt his lips claim the last words she spoke. It was a long ride home.

Roger called just as they entered her apartment and the news that he was finally coming over made her decide to postpone her own good news for just a bit. She wanted to be alone with Hawk when she told him about the baby. Something that special needed to be shared in very small increments, especially with first-time fathers. So she waited.

"Roger, where have you been?" Sara hissed. She yanked her brother by the arm, dragging him into the apartment.

"I had paperwork, you know, stuff." He shrugged in an offhand manner, hoping Sara would drop her line of questioning. "I didn't think you'd care." He walked into the living room where Hawk sat in darkness.

"Hey, old buddy, long time no see," Roger called out jovially. He was rewarded by a fierce, green stare that needed no artificial illumination to read.

Hawk turned back to Sara's television in stubborn silence.

"Boy!" Roger muttered. "What's the matter with him? I thought he'd be happier than this."

"He just saw my Wildcat commercial for the third time this evening," Sara whispered, trying to stifle a grin.

"Oh!" Roger nodded his head and mirrored his sister's

actions by stifling a grin, too. It had also taken him aback the first time he'd seen the commercial and she was only his sister.

"I think he'd gladly put me in a convent, for the rest of my born days, except then he couldn't have me either." Sara chuckled and ruffled Hawk's hair teasingly. "He just hasn't decided which emotion to give in to—jealousy or lust."

Roger took a seat by his former partner and clapped him on the back. "Well, old buddy," he said, "I can tell you from experience, you've got your hands full. Welcome to the family."

"From the look of that damn commercial, I don't have enough hands to even start," Hawk muttered.

He glared at Roger, trying to maintain his indignation in the face of all the ribald teasing, but his good nature won out. Laughing at himself, he pulled Sara down beside him and kissed her.

It was much later that evening before Hawk noticed something was not as it should be. Roger had used the phone continuously and never spoke above a whisper or mumble when they were in the room.

Hawk had been watching Roger for nearly an hour. All during dinner he had noticed something was bothering him and he was doing a poor job of hiding his distraction. Hawk had been on too many assignments with Roger not to read the signs. Sara was in the kitchen cleaning up the last of the dinner dishes when he decided he'd had enough. Hawk pinned a hard, green stare on Roger's fidgeting body and blurted out, "I'm tired of watching you play this game. Something's wrong. Don't try to deny it, just spit it out. Is it the thought of Sara . . . and me?"

"No!" Roger answered quickly, astonished that Hawk would even imagine such things. "Why would you even think that of me, Hawk? I thought we were better friends than this."

"Okay," Hawk sighed, determined to get to the source of Roger's problem. He had an ugly feeling it concerned him, regardless of Roger's assurances. "Then if it's not me, what in hell is it?"

Roger looked over his shoulder, taking note of his sister's whereabouts before he answered, and when he did the bottom fell out of Hawk's world.

"We can't find his body."

Hawk forgot to breath. His mind refused to accept who Roger must mean. He had to be referring to something . . . or someone else.

"Whose body?" he growled, but he knew the answer before it left Roger's mouth.

"Levette's. The Bandits have been all over the side of the mountain where he fell. There are signs of the fall, torn pieces of clothing, blood—but no body. We're going on the assumption that animals may have dragged it away. Unfortunately, Colonel Harris doesn't close a case on assumptions, so my men are still searching."

Hawk buried his face in his hands and then yanked them away, pushing himself upright from the sofa with an angry motion. He stood and walked slowly toward the window overlooking a magnificent view of downtown Dallas.

The lights outlining the skyline and the ones sprinkled throughout various skyscrapers mirrored the night sky on the Kiamichi—dark velvet sprinkled with stars, spilling out onto the curtain of night like yellow diamonds. But he didn't see the beauty or similarites as he tried to assimilate the enormities of Roger's statements.

But this makes sense, Hawk thought. *This is why I don't feel settled. It isn't over yet.*

"Have you ever considered the possibility that he may not be dead?"

Roger's face dropped and he ran a hand wearily across his eyes, pinching the bridge of his nose with his thumb and forefinger.

"I haven't thought of much else since I found out," he mumbled and sank into an overstuffed chair, burying his face in his hands.

Hawk's mind raced, sorting through the options Levette may have discovered. The Kiamichi was a world apart from this city. Just like the dark alleyways and abandoned buildings a city such as Dallas would have for a man to get lost in, the Kiamichi also had its secrets. There were hidden caves and ledges, trees so thick a man could not walk between them, creeks and rivers with deep holes that never saw the light of day. The bastard could be anywhere.

Hawk turned, laying his hand on Roger's shoulder as his voice echoed low and weary into the silence of the room,

"Give me tonight with Sara. I'll be waiting for you at the airport at dawn."

"No way, man!" Roger shouted, jumping back from the window and out of Hawk's reach as if his distance could emphasize his words more clearly. "This isn't your problem anymore. You've already contributed more than your share toward this operation. And besides, I know how you feel about the Company. They dealt you a blow even I can't forget." Roger's voice lowered and he stepped back toward his ex-partner, looking deeply into his eyes as he continued. "I didn't know they suspected Marla. I would have told you, Hawk, I swear," Roger muttered. "They used you just as they used my sister.

And both times I stood aside and let them do it because it was ordered."

A steady string of curses fell from Roger's lips as he paced back and forth in front of Hawk, his posture as stiff and uncompromising as the words he spoke. "Well, old buddy, there comes a time when orders have to take a backseat to what is right. Anyway, you're in no shape to slide around on that damn mountain."

Hawk's answer rumbled into the silence of the room. "It isn't for the Company. This is for me. If Levette is alive, he's mine."

Roger's respect for his ex-partner deepened at the enormity of the sacrifice Hawk was making by going back to the Kiamichi. He was in no shape to be climbing over the rough rock and wood terrain of the Kiamichi, but he knew that was not even a factor in Hawk's decision. Hawk needed to see for himself. He needed to bury his past, and the only way he was going to be able to do that was to bury Levette.

Roger nodded slowly, accepting Hawk's decision, and promised him everything he needed for the operation.

"My men are at your disposal. I'll be there, but you run the show, old friend. We're in your territory. If Levette's alive or dead, you'll find him."

Sara choked back the scream forcing its way up her throat and grabbed the side of the door for support as she overheard the last bit of Hawk and Roger's conversation. *Dear God, no!* she thought. *This can't be happening. It's just a bad dream.* But the truth she saw on their faces when they saw her standing in the doorway made her heart stop.

Damn! Hawk groaned. *How am I going to find the strength to leave her?*

Roger clasped Hawk's hand, quietly agreed on a meeting time and left the apartment, unable to look at his sister's stricken face.

Hawk started toward Sara when she shook her head in denial, speech impossible, and stumbled toward the refuge of her bedroom.

Hawk ran a weary hand across his face, wincing as his injuries protested against the deep breath he drew. He followed Sara to her room.

The light from the hallway left a pie-shaped slice of yellow on the carpet. Except for that, the room was in darkness. Hawk blinked several times, allowing his eyes to adjust to the shadows and finally he saw Sara standing at the window, leaning her head against the cold glass of the mullioned panes. He walked silently across the carpeted floor until he was so close he could feel her pain. Leaning his forehead against the back of her head, he inhaled the scented fragrance of her shampoo and the essence that was Sara. Sliding his arms about her, he pulled her against his chest, hugging her gently to him.

Then it seemed to Sara that the floodgates of Hawk's buried past cracked, and everything poured from him; all the guilt, all the bitterness, all the hate . . . and all the fear.

"I know Roger told you about Marla, but you need to hear it from me, baby," he whispered harshly. "She had black, curly hair and eyes so dark you couldn't see their pupils. There was a dimple in her right cheek and . . . her favorite ice cream was strawberry. The kind with chunks of real fruit in it. She was beautiful and brilliant . . . and made all the wrong choices in life. Her last one cost her dearly. She took a bullet meant for me and died in my arms." Then his voice broke and he buried his face against Sara's hair.

She felt him shaking as he let the anger and grief buried too long inside overwhelm him.

"I hated her . . . and I loved her. At least I loved who I thought she was. Marla was, after all, a consummate actress. She had me right where Levette wanted me. He suspected all along that I was an agent. She merely confirmed it," he muttered. "He just didn't expect Marla to have second thoughts about blowing me from the face of the earth."

Hawk's voice was deep and rough as he struggled with emotions the telling had unleashed. Sara started to turn and face Hawk but he resisted, it was as if he needed the emotional privacy of speaking to Sara, but not her watching him bare his soul.

Instantly, Sara understood and relented with a sigh. Hawk hugged her gently to him as he continued. "At the last moment, she looked at me and I swear to God I saw regret, but it was too late. I already knew her for what she really was. I would never have trusted her again and she knew it. Jesus, Sara," Hawk whispered, "she deliberately stepped in front of me as Levette shot. I still remember the look on Levette's face as he realized what she'd done . . . and I remember how it felt as Marla died in my arms. If I hadn't had Old Woman's failing health to contend with so soon afterward, I don't know . . ."

Sara started to speak, but Hawk forestalled her by finally turning her in his arms and capturing her lips; returning time and again to draw from her strength and sweetness. Then his whisper nearly broke Sara's heart.

"I've lived with this hate and betrayal so long, its nearly destroyed me. And then, little Wildcat, there was you. Losing you *would* destroy me. Please understand, Sara. If he's alive, you'll never be safe; not as long as you live."

Hawk cupped her face in his hands, capturing the tears on her cheeks with his thumbs, then laid her gently on the bed and loved her fears away.

The green luminescent number on the digital clock by Sara's bed made it easy for her to read the time; 2:05 A.M. She sat cross-legged in the middle of her bed, unconscious of her nudity, and watched Mackenzie Hawk sleep.

The central heating in her apartment made sleeping under heavy covers unnecessary and so he slept comfortably with only a light sheet and blanket for warmth, most of which was kicked off or twisted underneath him.

Sara's gaze feasted greedily on the hard, muscled perfection of his uncovered body.

This is the way I first saw him, she thought, remembering his near-nude state as she regained consciousness her first night on the Kiamichi, *and this is the way I'll remember him*. Then she pressed trembling fingers to her lips, choking back a cry and silently scolded herself for the turn her thoughts had taken. *I'm acting as if I'll never see him again, and I don't believe that. I can't. I could stop him from going. All I have to do is tell him about our baby.* But she didn't. And so it is with the way of women who love their men beyond measure. Sara gave Hawk the ultimate sacrifice—her silence.

An irresistible urge made Sara lean forward, lightly pressing her lips to the part of him that was hurt. Unable to stop at the bandages, Sara touched and tasted, tiny butterfly tastes of all that was Hawk. She didn't know he was awake until she heard his sharply indrawn breath as she touched his swelling manhood. She paused. He did not stop her, but lay silently, letting her do as she chose. Sara sighed as she leaned forward, her lips teased, her hands stroked, her tongue tasted. Not an inch of Hawk's body was overlooked as Sara brought him to fever-pitched torment. She felt the muscles of his thighs twitch and heard his breathing quicken as she increased her caresses.

Hawk was hard, aching, nearly to a bursting point as he struggled to maintain his sanity. The sight of her ivory beauty, the velvety feel of her skin as she touched and pushed against him . . . and her mouth. Oh God, her mouth . . . on his body. He groaned and moved, trying to pull Sara into position and let him into the depths of her womanhood, but she resisted.

It was so sudden, the wild flood of sensations that nearly lifted him from the bed. White pinpoints of light burst into a million pieces behind his eyelids. His body arched, and the muscles in his neck tightened and bowed as a cry from the depths of his soul called her name.

Hawk reached blindly down and buried his hands in her hair. Spasm after spasm racked his body until he feared there would be nothing left of him. It was minutes before his heart stopped pounding as though it was trying to escape from his chest. It was even longer before he could think coherently. All he could do was hold Sara cradled tightly against his chest and hope he didn't die from the pleasure she had so lovingly and unselfishly given him.

"My God!" he whispered hoarsely as he shakily touched Sara's face.

He saw he eyes glistening and saw the tender smile on her face, transforming it into an etheral beauty that made him feel the need to kneel at her feet. She was magnificent, his woman.

"Sara . . . Sara, how I love you. You're the best part of all that I am," he declared unsteadily.

Sara nodded, unable to speak as she accepted his tribute.

"I promise you . . . on everything holy, I'll be back. You hear me, baby? I promise you."

He pulled her fiercely into his arms and hugged her, ignoring the warning twinges from his injured ribs.

Sara finally slept, cradled within the safety of Mackenzie Hawk. When she awoke hours later, the digital clock read 8:47 A.M. and he was gone.

It was then Sara cried.

"Right here, Hawk. This is where we lost the trail," Lieutenant Travis pointed.

The Bandits had been over and over the area where Levette fell and the only definite signs still readable ended right where Travis was indicating. The Tennessee Bandit was proving to be the best tracker in the outfit. His sharpshooter eyesight missed very little of the signs Hawk had instructed the men to look for.

Hawk grunted as he knelt down to inspect the long indentations in the thick layer of rotting leaves and tree bark. His injuries had not bothered him as much as he'd feared. Maybe it was just coming back to the Kiamichi. It had once healed his soul, possibly it healed bodies as well.

He shrugged in disgust and checked the surrounding area, again. They'd been looking a day and a night and hadn't come any closer to finding a clue as to Levette's whereabouts. Was he dead or was the evil bastard hiding, waiting for an opportunity to take another soul with him into hell?

The weather was holding and Hawk was profoundly grateful for the small favor. If it snowed again, what few signs still visible would be lost.

"Someone crawled through here," he said, pointing toward a deep tangle of underbrush. "Those aren't drag marks as you first suspected, Roger. See . . . there . . . the dish-shaped impressions here and here. They were made by the heel of a man's hand.''

Roger whistled softly. Hawk knew his stuff. That ruled out the theory of animals dragging off a body.

"Damn," he muttered, pacing nervously as he looked upward, gauging the distance of Levette's fall. "How do you survive a thing like that? I know the brush probably slowed the fall, but he's shot. I know that. That's what knocked him off the mountain.''

"It's hard to kill evil," Hawk answered, and walked toward the dense growth where the marks disappeared. Suddenly he stopped, sensing movement from deep within the brambles.

"Be careful, Hawk," Roger warned and quickly drew the gun from his holster. "Get back!" he ordered. "Travis . . .''

The unspoken order was understood as Lt. Travis trained his sights on the rustling noises that were growing louder.

Then the brush parted and a grey shadow bounded from the underbrush.

"Don't shoot!" Hawk shouted and dropped to his knees as Dog pounced happily about, seemingly overjoyed to find his master.

Hawk grabbed his pet roughly by the hair on his neck and pulled him close. Dog's shaggy winter coat was all matted and small brambles clung persistently to his wildly thrashing tail.

"You old maverick," Hawk said, combing his hands through the thick, winter fur, pulling out briars and bits of leaves. "I suppose you want me to believe you've been looking all over for me. I haven't seen you in days, old boy. Where were you when I needed you?''

Hawk grinned at the comical expression on Dog's face and gave him one last pat as he slowly got to his feet. Dog raced ahead, tongue lolling from his mouth, as he headed for home and food.

"False alarm, boy. This one is a menace to rabbits and lady wolves only."

Laughter broke the tension as the men decided to call it a day. It was less than an hour to sunset and they still had to get back up the mountain to Hawk's cabin. It was being used for headquarters and the Company men had no complaints about the change of address. It was a lot better than the one-man pup tents they'd roosted in for nearly a week before the showdown with Levette had occurred.

The men's voices carried through the lowering temperature and rising altitude as they neared the cabin. It was obvious they were ready for some food and rest but Hawk was getting desperate. He felt an overwhelming need to get home to Sara as quickly as possible and it didn't look likely to happen any time soon. His thoughts were scattered like leaves in a whirlwind. This search could go on forever if Levette was alive. There were too many places to hide. And, if he was dead, it could still take weeks, even months to find him. There had to be a better way.

Most of the Bandits had been together since the beginning and they traded old stories of remember whens before the roaring fire Hawk provided. But they did little to stop the aching loneliness that kept pushing and pushing at Hawk. Here he was, back in the place he'd grown up in with a house full of people and he was so lonely he wanted to cry. He missed Sara's cold feet in the bend of his knees at night. He missed her stubbornness, her laughter . . . Hell, he even missed the fits.

"I'm going to get some air," he muttered to no one in particular and started outside.

"Man, it's too cold for sightseeing," one of the men called, but was silenced by a look from Roger Beaudry.

Roger knew his friend and suspected what drove him. He was going crazy with frustration himself. Harris was on his back day and night. He wanted to be finished with Levette, too.

Hawk walked silently, but with purpose, to the very edge of the mountain where he and Levette had struggled and where, but for Roger, he had nearly died.

His eyes blurred from the cold air as he stood unblinking, searching; searching the pitch black of the tree line that fell downward before him. All the while, hoping something would come to him that would tell him how to find that bastard. Hawk burned with an anger so deep, so old, he knew it had to go out before he could ever go back to Sara. She didn't deserve his old ghosts.

Hawk was gone so long, Roger was beginning to worry and sensed the other men's anxiety as well. Finally, he nodded his okay for the Tennessee Bandit to check outside and make sure all was well.

The men silently followed Travis outside and were stopped, stunned mute by the sight of Mackenzie Hawk standing at the mountain's precipice. He stood arms raised, fists clenched, as if in defiance at the mountain that had his adversary and the moonlight that only half lit the secrets on the Kiamichi. Then, before any of them could speak, Hawk's voice rang out over the mountain and the hair stood on each of the men's necks at the rage with which Hawk called Levette's name.

The name echoed into the night and down, down the mountain until it came ricocheting back, defiant in spite of the muted, faded sound.

The men were stunned by the sound, but nothing prepared them for the answer that followed, clear and cutting the stillness of the mountain with stunning clarity.

At first it had sounded like the wind, far off, whistling eerily through the trees, but it began to gain strength and sound and momentum. Finally, it filled the darkness all about them in one long, tormented howl of mortal anguish. On and on it lasted and the men held their breath, afraid to speak for fear of alerting the devil that had uttered the sound. Then there was silence.

Hawk threw back his head, letting the sound flow over him and through him and he sighed. Now he knew for certain his work was still undone.

Turning, he walked back toward the cabin, barely glancing up at the men who stood in stunned silence.

"Jesus!" one of them finally whispered as they followed Hawk inside. "What in hell was that . . . a wolf or big cat or something?"

Hawk turned quietly to face the crowd of men awaiting an answer.

"Levette is alive," he whispered, his lack of emotion ominous by omission, and he missed the looks of apprehension on their faces as he went to his solitary bed.

"It won't be long now, Levette," he said aloud, just before exhaustion pulled him into a deep, dreamless sleep. "I know how to find you now."

The next morning his manner was not at all what Roger or the Bandits expected. This purposeful man striding about from room to room, making lists and drawing maps was not the same frustrated man of yesterday. And then he announced, "Roger, we've been going about this search all wrong."

"What do you mean?"

"Levette is a sociopath, an animal. Actually, he's a wounded animal."

"So?" Roger said, having trouble following Hawk's new line of thought.

"So, when animals get hurt, they hole up. They hide during the day because that's when they feel the most vulnerable. But when night falls, if they are able, they come out and forage, secure in the shadows."

"Well, Christ, man! You mean we are going to have to walk this damn mountain in the dark?"

"Not exactly," Hawk said. "But we can set a trap that might draw him out."

"You mean a steel-tooth, bear-type trap?"

"No, I mean a city trap. Levette is a city dweller. He can't know much about wilderness survival. He's been without comforts for days now and he's hurt. I'd wager right about now he's as desperate as he's ever been in his life.

"But how do we set this trap if he only comes out at night?"

"That's the easy part. Come on," Hawk called as he started outside. "We've got a little planning to do. Roger, old buddy, you're going to have a terrible accident on your way home today and scatter your groceries all the the way down the Kiamichi. It's a damn shame, too. Those steaks cost a fortune." Hawk laughed at the look of dismay on Roger's face.

The Bandits were in position as dusk lengthened the shadows on the mountain. The area where the wreck had been faked was not far from the area where Levette had fallen over the mountain. It was conceivable that he had strayed farther away, but Hawk thought it unlikely.

They used Sara's motorcycle. Hawk felt no remorse as he watched it bounce end over end down the side of the mountain. If he had any say in the matter, she'd never ride anything like it again. He got sick everytime he thought about her ride up the mountain the night they met.

Hawk watched in satisfaction as groceries scattered all down the mountainside and the cycle added its own bit of drama to the situation by exploding into flames near the bottom. The fire was a bonus. Levette would be drawn to the warmth as well as the food. An hour passed as the moon rose over the Kiamichi, casting its yellow glow through the dense brush. The temperature dropped as a few wispy clouds drifted across the sky, scattering into the atmosphere like tattered lace. Hawk watched, his eyes narrowed to green slits as he searched the play of shadows throughout the forest. Smoke from the wreck drifted into his eyes and made them water. *The wind has changed*, he thought. He blinked quickly, trying to clear his vision and almost missed it. Movement! On the other side of the wreck he saw . . . his heart quickened. Adrenaline pumped into his system, readying for the confrontation.

Something was disturbing the floor of the forest as the scent of cold, rotting leaves filled the air. It mingled with the faint smoke traces and another more subversive scent. He waited.

The explosion rocked the silence of the mountain. The creature jumped, clasping a hand to its ear to block out the sound. The sudden movement sent fresh pain rocketing through its body. A shrill, feral cry escaped its mouth. Soon, the odor of smoke drifted through the dense undergrowth that was hiding the opening of the abandoned wolf den. The creature's nostrils quivered and flared. A faint memory tried to surface. Smoke meant fire—and fire meant warmth. And it was cold, so cold.

It crawled weakly to the opening and peered through the tangle of brush. The light was almost gone but the smoke trail remained. The creature crawled through the low opening and painfully pulled itself upright. One arm hung limply at its side; useless, shattered from . . . something. It couldn't remember. Just pain . . . day into night . . . into another day . . . there was only pain and hunger and cold in its world.

It began the slow, arduous journey toward the origin of the smoke, its feet dragging weakly through the dense carpet of wet debris lining the forest floor. As it drew nearer, another more enticing odor reached its nostrils. It stopped and sniffed the wind like the animal it had become. It sensed food. Something from long ago . . . before the pain. Not the bark and dead leaves that had served as food and warmth. Not the dead foliage it had sucked on for succor and more than once choked on.

It lumbered into the small burned space where the upside-down skeleton of the Harley rested. Torn cellophane on the packages of scattered groceries gleamed in the moonlight and allowed their scents to seep enticingly into the night air. It stumbled wildly toward the aroma, caution forgotten as it tore ravenously into food and paper alike.

Little grunts as it chewed and smacked, frantically smearing the food over its face and into its mouth told the stunned men, as nothing else could have, of the deterioration of their prey.

The Bandits began emerging quietly from their hiding places, moving toward Levette as he crawled from one treasure to another, cramming raw and cooked food alike into his mouth.

The men ringed the creature, allowing him room to forage, but this time, there would be no escape.

Levette continued tearing wildly into package after package as he filled a belly too-long empty.

Hawk and Roger watched as what was left of Levette scoured the damp ground for more food.

"My God!" Roger muttered, watching Levette move fully into a moonlit patch of ground.

The beautiful, golden countenance was gone. Surface beauty had eroded into the evil and ugliness that had been Levette. He wore hideous bruises, deep gashes in his face and hands, broken bones; all remnants of his fall from the mountain.

Hawk watched in grim satisfaction. All need for revenge was cleansed from his soul as he saw the creature crawling about, oblivious to the audience. He felt no remorse for Levette's terrible injuries, for he was remembering other faces, and other times. A girl with dark, laughing eyes and a beautiful redhead with one side of her face shredded raw.

"Like this, Levette escapes our justice," Hawk said, his voice low and distinct. "But he didn't escape a higher justice. The Kiamichi did what we could not. This," he gestured toward the creature, "will never escape from the living hell inside his head."

He turned, suddenly very weary and very lonely for Sara. The Bandits could have what was left of Levette. He walked away, disappearing into the night shadows on the Kiamichi.

TWELVE

The day after Hawk left, Sara wept copious tears of fear and frustration. Only a pounding headache and no more tissues convinced her to stop. She had refused to answer the phone because of the news media and then worried excessively that she might have missed a call from Hawk. A very unobtrusive guard hovered about in her hallway, preventing unwelcome visitors but he also discouraged any that might have helped her pass the time.

The next day, Sara put the answering machine on the phone, gave out three interviews to local papers, made plans to meet with Morty to discuss what was left of her career and how to salvage or end it, and refused an invitation to a local talk show.

She was tired of hiding. Levette had been the cause of her disappearance from Dallas, now he was the cause of her enforced inactivity in Dallas and she was frustrated beyond belief. The only thing that was going to make everything right in Sara's world was a phone call from Hawk, and until it came, she was putting everything on hold.

"I should have heard something by now," Sara muttered, guilt and nerves warring inside her brain until she feared she would go mad. "I shouldn't have let him go. I could have stopped him." Then she sighed as she looked longingly out the window, "And he would have hated me later."

Sara turned away from the window and walked to the bed before dropping down to the fluffy comforter in despair. She turned about on the bed and faced her own reflection in the mirror over her dresser.

From a distance, if she squinted her eyes just right, she couldn't tell she'd ever been injured. That told her one thing. She could work again if she wanted. But there was Hawk . . . and their baby . . . to consider. Her heart told her they were all that was ever going to matter again in her life. She opened her eyes wider and looked again in the mirror, this time she saw the woman, not the model. She stood, let her bathrobe fall from her shoulders to a silken puddle on the carpet.

This is also me, Sara thought, eyeing her high, full-breasted figure, tiny waist, and slender hips. The long-limbed beauty of her body was what had made her famous. That . . . and her hair. Sara grabbed her mane into a wad at the nape of her neck and turned, looking at herself fully from every angle. And then her knees grew weak and her hands shook as she remembered. There wasn't a square inch of her body that Hawk hadn't touched, kissed, claimed for his own.

Sara, independent, do-it-herself woman of the 90's no longer belonged just to herself. A very large, very important part of her world now belonged to Mackenzie Hawk and the baby they had been made from their love. Until he returned, she could not, would not, make any decisions about Sara Beaudry.

And if the waiting wasn't enough, not knowing if Hawk was still in danger, Sara also discovered by way of a very harried accountant, who presented himself at her door the same evening, that Mackenzie Hawk was a fraud.

Sara was furious. The accountant finally left with Sara's promise that Hawk would call him the moment he returned to Dallas. Sara practically slammed the door in his face as she hastened his exit.

"How dare Hawk hide something like this from me? He deceived me into thinking he was living on the mountain because he couldn't afford to live elsewhere. At least that's what I thought," Sara muttered to herself as she flung pillows and magazines about in the apartment. She was working herself into at least an 8.7 on the Richter scale for fits.

"He's not the poor, misunderstood Indian who hid himself on the Kiamichi because the Company and the world dumped on him. No!" she shouted to no one in particular. "He's a very wealthy, misunderstood Indian, and one of his investments just put him into a higher tax bracket."

She flopped down in a chair, rested her head in her hands, and allowed tears of frustration to fall unchecked.

"Oh God," she prayed, "I just want him back. Then I'll deal with the underhanded sucker my own way."

A familiar sound penetrated Sara's sleep and she pulled the pillow from her head, cracking one sleepy eye toward the window.

"No, not raining," she mumbled, and turned over on her back, trying to identify the sound. "Shower . . . that's what it is. Must have left the shower running."

She pulled the T-shirt she was sleeping in down from its wad around her neck and rolled back up into her cocoon, satisfied she had correctly identified the sound.

It took approximately three seconds for the stupidity of her own remark to reach her brain.

"I don't leave showers running!" she said, threw back the covers and stumbled sleepily toward the bathroom.

Her heart beat double-time as she saw a familiar pile of clothing on the bathroom floor.

"Hawk!" She yanked open the shower door and bounded inside, letting steam and water out onto the walls and floor of the room.

"Darling, you're back. Thank God! Are you all right? Is it over?" She threw her arms about his neck and began raining tiny kisses all over his naked body.

One very wet, very surprised Indian grinned from ear to ear at the sight he beheld. He reached over and slid the shower door shut as he wrapped Sara in a giant hug.

"Hi, baby," he whispered. "I didn't mean to wake you." He couldn't wipe the silly grin from his face. "You look adorable," he announced and captured her mouth with his lips. She tasted wonderful . . . all wet and soft and tempting.

He reluctantly pulled away from her kiss. "You're all wet, little Wildcat. And I must say, I've never seen a wet cat look better. Look at you!"

Sara's T-shirt was plastered to every minute curve of her body, and her hair hung down her back like wet silk. Thousands of tiny, tear-like droplets from the shower mist coated every bare inch of her skin, clinging like heavy dewdrops after an early morning shower.

"No," Sara said softly, as she reached down and peeled the T-shirt upwards from her body, reveling in the green fire she lit in Hawk's eyes as she performed her mini-striptease. "Look at you."

Bronzed muscles flexed and rippled, from the width of his shoulders to the lean waist, narrow hips, and down the long length of his legs and feet. Hawk could not hide the rising evidence of his desire for Sara.

"That's cheating," he groaned.

Sara slipped her arms around his neck and leaned into him. "You shouldn't be so sexy, Indian," Sara said.

Some bruising was still evident on his ribcage, and Sara bent down and kissed the hurts. His body was warm and slick from soap and shampoo and Sara's hands slid over it like silk over steel.

Hawk laughed aloud as Sara stepped under the full force of the water and came out sputtering. She started to retaliate by giving him a dose of the same medicine but Hawk resisted. Instead, hard muscles in his arms and shoulders bunched. He grabbed Sara and pulled her about, pinning her against the shower wall and let the warm spray and mist pepper both their bodies like tiny kneading fingers of heat. He ached. His loins throbbed with need for Sara. He groaned, feeling her body as it moved and teased against him.

"Sara. Wait, baby," he pleaded, and felt her hands working familiar magic.

He was desperately trying to get Sara out of the shower and into the bed.

"I don't want to wait," Sara whispered, nipping sharply at his earlobe.

"If that's what you want," he said, his voice low and promising in the warmth and seclusion of their tiny world, "then that's what you get."

Hawk drove his aching body into Sara and felt the world spin. Over and over he thrust, trying to bury himself so deeply, he would never find his way back. He felt Sara's muscles tense, felt her body convulse in tiny tremors around him as he took her. The sensation was addictive. He couldn't get enough.

"Hawk, please," Sara begged. She never wanted this feeling to stop, but she needed it to end. "No more . . . please. Oh, God!" she gasped, and would have fallen had Hawk not held her so tightly against him. The earth spun off its axis as Hawk took Sara over the edge into oblivion.

Hawk's legs felt like rubber, and his heart was pounding like a jackhammer. He'd never been so weak, or felt so good in his life.

"Oh, baby," he groaned, slowly regaining his equilibrium. "You take everything out of me."

That phrase triggered Sara's memory as Hawk turned off the water and helped Sara step out of the shower. She walked slowly into the bedroom, his words pounding at her conscience, and she fumbled in her dresser for another nightshirt.

"Yep, I took it all right," Sara mumbled, referring to her pregnant state, "and kept it."

"What did you say?" Hawk asked from the bathroom as he gathered up his and Sara's wet clothing and headed toward the laundry.

"Nothing," Sara said, suddenly hesitant to tell Hawk of her delicate condition. She needed to pick just the right time.

She looked at herself in the full-length mirror hanging on the back of the closet door. "I don't look any different. I wonder if Hawk will notice," she said to herself, and splayed her fingers across her flat stomach.

"Notice what?" Hawk asked as he walked back into the room.

"Uh, notice if I'm not dressed."

"Only if I go blind and die, baby," he growled, pulling her against him.

"Come to bed, silly," Sara whispered, and pulled back

the bedcovers. "It's hours until morning. Let's get some rest. You can tell me about Levette tomorrow."

"There's not much to tell," Hawk said. "The Kiamichi succeeded where we failed. It's over."

Hawk lay down, sinking wearily into the bed's warmth and comfort.

Sara saw his exhaustion as muscles relaxed and he quietly closed his eyes. She crawled closer, laid her head on his shoulder and wrapped herself around him.

The last thought Hawk remembered as he let exhaustion and sleep claim him was, *It feels so good to be home.*

Sara lay against his heartbeat, and for the first time since he'd gone back to the Kiamichi, she slept a deep, dreamless sleep.

"Listen, mister," Sara gritted through tightly clenched teeth, trying to keep her voice and blood pressure down. "I told you I'd have Mackenzie Hawk call. If I said he'll call you, he'll call. But you're not talking to him now because he's still asleep."

Sara was glaring at the accountant from yesterday who had made a return trip. And he wasn't any too pleased with Sara Beaudry either.

"Please, Miss Beaudry. I know he's asleep, but this is the last day of the year, and tomorrow will be too late. These business transactions must be completed before the New Year. Tax purposes, you know. I must insist."

"You do what you must," Sara argued. "I'm still not waking him up."

The accountant's face was as red as Sara's hair. He'd never in his life met such an obstinate woman.

Hawk awakened to the sound of angry voices coming from the living room. He crawled from the bed into a pair of Levis, and walked into the ensuing argument. "Sara, what in hell is all the fuss about?"

"Now, see what you have done," Sara said to the accountant, her eyes as accusing as the tone of her voice.

A very relieved man spied the object of his search sauntering barefoot into the living room. "Mr. Hawk, thank goodness," he cried.

"Hanley!" Hawk said, surprise evident in his demeanor. "What are you doing here? More to the point, how did you even know where to find me?"

Hawk came up behind Sara and casually slid his arm around her shoulders as he spoke.

Well! Sara thought. *He doesn't seem to mind that I've met this little worm. Maybe this isn't such a big secret after all.*

"I wouldn't be bothering you if you'd just answered any one of my last five letters," Hanley accused. He made himself comfortable and opened his briefcase. "I saw you on TV the other night. Couldn't believe my eyes, or my luck. There you were in living color, bruises and all and right here in Dallas."

"Letters?" Hawk echoed, and then remembering the chaos of the last few weeks he sighed and ran his hand through his hair. "I haven't been to the post office in nearly a month. I've been a bit . . . preoccupied. Sorry."

Hanley raised his eyebrows and looked pointedly at Sara.

"Indeed," he drawled. "If you didn't insist on living in the wilds, or if you would at least make an appearance at my office once in a while, this type of crisis wouldn't come up."

"So, what's the problem," Hawk asked, and grinned at Sara's indignant expression. *She must really be miffed about this. But for the life of me I can't figure out why,* he thought.

He pulled Sara down beside him as he sat across the table from his accountant. The man was a genius, but he was never going to live to be a hundred. He worried too much.

"I didn't know you had an accountant, sweetheart," Sara cooed, her eyes flashing angrily. "In fact, I didn't even know you needed one."

Ahh, Hawk thought, *the light dawns.* He merely grinned and turned his attention to Hanley. *Let her stew a bit. Maybe then she'll understand how I felt when I saw her Wildcat commercials. I suspect we're both still due a few shocks about each other.*

"What's so urgent?" Hawk prompted.

Hanley sighed in relief and dug through the depths of his briefcase, pulling out a handful of papers as he regained control of the situation on familiar territory—business.

"You have until 6:00 P.M. today to decide if you want to sell *Little Red* to a New York conglomerate. They want to franchise all over the Southwest and that's just for starters."

"Who are they and what's their offer?" Hawk asked, his voice clipped and decisive. His eyes narrowed and his lips thinned, as yet another facet of his personality emerged.

Sara sat in shocked silence, observing the man before her as he fielded the questions Hanley threw at him with obvious expertise. *Sell Little Red?* Sara thought. *One of Dallas' hottest nightspots . . . then that means he owns it. For heaven's sake, what else is he hiding?*

Hawk's raised eyebrows were the only indication of his feelings as the accountant quoted the buyer's offer. Sara's mouth dropped open and it was with great effort that she managed to close it without a shriek. How many millions? She jumped to her feet, suddenly very, very nauseated.

"Excuse me," she murmured, and made a mad dash for the bathroom.

Hawk took one startled look at Sara's face and bolted after her. He'd seen that look before.

Hanley flopped the papers down and leaned back in disgust. This was proving to be more difficult with each passing moment. His wife would kill him if he missed the New Year's Eve party. She had a new dress . . . hired a babysitter . . . Lord! At this rate, he'd never be home on time.

"Sara, what's wrong?" Hawk asked, as he grabbed a towel and handed it to her as she leaned over the sink and splashed her face and neck with icy water.

"Ummmm, shock, I suppose," Sara muttered. Now was not the time to talk about morning sickness.

"Sweetheart, I'm sorry," Hawk said and pulled her hair away from her face and neck, helping her blot the water from her clothes. "All this wasn't meant to be a secret. We've merely done all this backwards. We fell in love . . . and made love . . . before I even knew if you liked mustard or mayonnaise."

He planted a gentle kiss on the top of her head, regretting the look of bewilderment on Sara's face that he knew he was responsible for.

"I know," Sara said, and choked back a hiccup. "I'm just being silly. I've never judged a man by the size of his bank balance." Then she leaned her head into his chest as Hawk wrapped her in a hug, cuddling her against his bare flesh. "It's just . . ."

"What, baby," he asked, his voice low and coaxing as he gently smoothed down her flyaway curls.

"It's true I've never judged a man by his bank balance, but I also never expected to love a man who owned the whole darn bank either."

Hawk threw back his head and roared with laughter. "Sara, Sara, I love you. You're absolutely priceless. Come lie down until you feel better," Hawk ordered, and led her gently toward the bed. "The sooner I finish my business with Hanley, the sooner he'll be gone. It won't take long."

"What are you going to do . . . about selling, I mean?" Sara asked a moment later, grinning sheepishly as Hawk tucked her into bed. She couldn't stand the suspense and patience was not one of her better attributes.

"Sell, of course," he answered.

"Why?"

"Because, I don't want you to be cheated out of your bank, little Wildcat." He grinned at the embarrassed look on her face, leaned down and brushed her lips with a predatory kiss before he hurried back to the anxious accountant.

Sara dozed off and when she awoke, it was midmorning and Hawk was nowhere in sight. However, a note taped to the bathroom mirror assured her he had not gone far.

Had to go sign papers. If you feel like it, I've made reservations at Little Red for New Year's Eve tonight. I'll bid farewell to Little Red and the old year at one time. I'm looking forward to the New Year and you. Wear something great . . . that requires underwear. See you later. Love, Me.

Sara peeled the note from the mirror and laughed. Hawk didn't talk as much as he wrote. Maybe they should communicate by letter more often. And she knew just what she would wear tonight. It would be too late for him to worry about underwear when she told him about the baby.

She had a feeling panties would be the last thing on his mind.

Sara yelped aloud as she tried to run a comb through the tangle of curls in her hair. Baby or not, rich or poor, she couldn't brush the damn tangles out of her hair by herself. Anyway she looked at it, she needed Mackenzie Hawk.

THIRTEEN

Hawk pushed the floor button in the elevator as the door slid shut. It had taken him a bit longer than he previously planned to finish his business. Then he'd made several other stops along the way home and he was late. He wanted tonight to be very special for Sara. He grinned to himself as he fiddled with the bags under his arms. Sara wasn't the only one full of surprises.

He shifted the heavy garment bag he was carrying to the other hand and slung it over his shoulder just as the elevator reached Sara's floor. Smoothing the hair on the back of his neck, he patted his jacket pocket, assuring himself the contents were still safely in place and stepped out of the elevator.

He heard the argument before he ever got close to Sara's apartment.

"What in the world?" he muttered, hurrying to her door. "It can't be Hanley again. I just left him."

Hawk opened the door quietly and slipped inside the hallway. Sara's rage was obvious, and the obsequious voice that kept interrupting her tirade belonged to . . .

"Morty," Sara argued, "I can't make a decision about it now. I don't even want to. How many times do I have to say that?"

"Sara . . . sweetheart. You know I only have your best interests at heart. But your contract is up tomorrow, and I thought we'd just renew now and save you the hassle on a holiday. It's been great so far . . . why rock the boat?"

Hawk was furious. He started to bolt into the room and tend to Morty in a manner he was certainly not acustomed to, but he hesitated, giving Sara time to deal with him in her own way. He read the nervous tone in Morty's voice. He wasn't half as concerned with Sara's welfare as he was his own. If she didn't renew her contract, he didn't get his ten percent.

"I need a rest," Sara answered. "That's why. I'm not even certain I want to work anymore."

"You can't afford to quit now, can you?" Morty sneered.

"What are you getting at?" Sara asked.

"That Indian you dug out of the Oklahoma hills . . . and decided to *keep*. He'll be costly."

The innuendo on the word "keep" sent Sara into hysterics. She broke into peals of laughter, gasping for breath between spasms. The few words she managed to say were incoherent.

Hawk sighed and smiled to himself. He wouldn't be in Morty's shoes for anything. Sara happy was one thing, Sara totally pissed off was something else entirely. And Hawk had a feeling Sara was just about at that point. He remained silent but ready to come to her aid should she need it.

"What's so funny?" Morty growled. He had a feeling

there was a lot more he should have researched before he began this conversation.

"Actually, nothing you've said so far is the least bit funny," Sara said, and flopped down on a bar stool by the cabinet where Morty had obligingly spread all the contract papers.

She shuffled them together, handed them to Morty, and wiped away tears of laughter with the tail of her blouse. "Here, Morty. Be thankful that all I'm giving you are your papers back. Believe me, it's not exactly what I'd like to do right now. Don't *ever* speak of Hawk again in such a derogatory manner. In fact, you'd be much better off, if you didn't even mention his name to me. Am I making myself clear?" The hard, angry tone in her voice hid nothing of her disgust for Morty's manner. "If I need a manager again, you'll be the first to know. But for now, don't call me. I'll call you."

Morty yanked the papers from her outstretched hands and stomped from the room, pausing only to grab his coat from the back of a chair. He headed toward the door and then his life flashed before his eyes as he saw Mackenzie Hawk leaning nonchalantly against the wall.

"How . . . how long have you been standing here?" Morty stammered. His heart tried to crawl out the toe of his shoes as Hawk answered.

"Too damn long for your health," Hawk said quietly.

"That's what I thought," Morty whispered, and edged toward the doorway and safety. He almost had it made when Hawk's menacing growl stopped him.

"Morty."

"Yeah?" he said weakly and closed his eyes.

"Don't come back."

"Yeah, right," he agreed and bolted for the door.

Hawk stood a moment longer, allowing a bit of time to pass before he walked into the living room.

"Hi, baby," Hawk said as he stepped silently into the room.

Sara dropped the pillow cushions from her hands, letting them fall in puffy disarray onto the sofa.

"Hawk?" Sara asked and tried to clear the squeak from her voice. "What have you done to yourself?"

"Nothing much. Just picked up a few clothes and got a haircut. Been needing one for weeks."

Sara nodded slowly, trying to adjust to the stranger standing before her. Then she focused on jade eyes and a familiar look of lust and sighed. *It's Hawk all right,* she thought, and watched hypnotized as the dark stranger lay down packages and bags and sauntered toward her.

"What's the matter, little Wildcat? Do you still feel bad?"

Sara shook her head in denial and ran her fingers through the closely cropped hair on the back of Hawk's neck. It sprang back into place, laying like an ebony cap as her fingers passed through its shortened length. A lock of hair fell across his forehead like a raven's wing, giving him a rakish, devil-may-care look. Coupled with grey, tailored slacks, a bulky fisherman's knit sweater, and a black leather bomber jacket, Sara thought he was drop-dead gorgeous.

"No, I feel fine," she finally answered.

"Great! Tonight has to be special. Just like you, little Wildcat."

He tangled his fingers in her hair, tilted her head to a perfect angle, and stole a kiss.

You have no idea, Sara thought, as she let Hawk's mouth work its own brand of magic. *It's going to be a night you'll never forget.*

*   *   *

The Wildcat darted through traffic as if a pack of dogs was on its trail.

"You drive remarkably like my brother," Sara said, as she tugged at her seat belt, assuring herself she was safely belted.

Hawk's answering grin and sardonic tilt to his eyebrow made Sara's heart skip a beat. He looked fantastic.

Mackenzie Hawk was a real sleeper. There were models who spent years trying to obtain the looks that Mackenzie Hawk took for granted and ignored.

When he'd pulled the custom-made tuxedo from the garment bag, Sara knew he was gearing up for what he thought was the grand finale to their courtship before moving on to the next, and more permanent phase of their relationship.

Sara nervously wiped her sweaty palms on the plush seat covers of her car as Hawk darted and swerved between the rushing cars traveling at usual breakneck speeds. However, it wasn't Hawk's driving that was making Sara nervous, it was how he was going to receive the news of their blessed event.

"We're here," he announced, swerving into a brightly lit parking lot as he stopped under the covered walk leading to the club.

"Good evening, sir," the parking attendant said, deftly catching the keys Hawk tossed his way.

"Evening, son," Hawk drawled, "park her gentle, she's been rode hard."

"Yes, sir," he grinned, playing along with Hawk's teasing remark.

Hawk ushered Sara inside the crowded lobby, past a long line of people waiting to get inside. Busy employees deftly dodged between standing and seated patrons alike as they scurried to deliver their heavily loaded trays of drinks. A live band was playing, adding to the pandemonium of New Year's Eve.

More than one pair of eyes turned at their passing, both male and female alike, for Mackenzie Hawk and Sara Beaudry made a striking couple. And they were news, even if it was just local Dallas news.

Sara heard the whispers and felt the stares. She'd lived with them for years, but this time it felt different. This time, she was just the teeniest bit jealous of the stares women were giving Hawk and she flashed them a proprietary look that brooked no interference.

He's mine, her eyes warned, *more than you'll ever know*.

"Right this way, Mr. Hawk," the waitress said, smiling bashfully at them as they reached their destination. "We all appreciate your consideration for the employees when you sold *Little Red*. I'm to thank you on behalf of all the workers for the assurance that none of us are to be replaced or fired."

"No problem, Shirley," Hawk said, as he seated Sara. Then he shook the girl's outstretched hand. "Just do a good job for the new owners like you did for me and you'll have nothing to worry about. Good luck!"

"Yes, sir, and good luck to you, too," she said, smiling pointedly at Sara.

Everyone at *Little Red* knew about their boss and the Texas Wildcat. In the employee's own small way, it was their one long-distance claim to fame.

Hawk watched Sara's gaze dart nervously about the crowded room and he wondered what was bothering her. He realized that this was the first time she had appeared in public since her accident, but she looked great. Something told him that wasn't why she was so quiet. Her face was so nearly healed, that unless he looked very hard, Hawk couldn't even tell where the injuries had been. It was the scars inside that were worrying Hawk. Maybe she was suffering some kind of delayed stress. That had been a tense situation on the Kiamichi, even for a seasoned agent. Sara just might be having problems tonight being around so many strangers. Hostage situations often produced very long term traumas for victims.

Hawk reached across the table and gently took away the napkin she was worrying into a wadded mess. Her hands were like ice and her fingers were actually shaking.

"Sara . . . baby. What's wrong?" he coaxed.

Sara looked at Hawk's face, so solemn and tense as he awaited an answer. She could only shake her head. If she spoke, she was afraid she would cry. She was so happy, she wanted him to receive their news with as much joy as she had and now that it was time to tell him, she didn't quite know how.

"Your dress is beautiful, little Wildcat," he said gently, "just like you. And I won't even check for underwear."

Sara's answering grin, weak though it was, tore at Hawk's heart. *What in hell*? he wondered. *Maybe she's changed her mind. It happened before,* he worried and then cautioned himself not to borrow imaginary trouble. Not Sara! She wouldn't ever let him down.

He rose from the table and walked around behind her chair, leaned over and whispered into her ear. "Dance with me, Sara."

Sara's heart skipped a beat. She recognized the tone of his voice and the exact words. She should. She'd used them herself when they were still at the cabin.

She rose from her seat and walked slowly ahead of Hawk onto the crowded dance floor. Turning, she melted into his arms, relishing the proprietary way he claimed his right to hold her.

Colored lights from the twisting globe suspended above the dance floor blinked rapidly, even into darkened corners of the room. Hawk whirled Sara across the floor, waltzing her carefully between tangled couples as skillfully as he maneuvered the car on the Dallas freeway.

The metallic sheen of her electric-blue evening dress reflected the frenzy of the evening's partygoers. It caught and held the reflections and shadows of everything shiny as Hawk waltzed Sara about the room.

Sara's dress, like Sara herself, was deceiving. It had long, fitted sleeves and a high neck. The fabric clung tightly to her graceful curves all the way to the juncture of her thighs before it flared wildly into folds and folds of blue down the length of her long legs to the tips of matching high-heeled shoes. Her hair fell into thousands of loose wayward curls, just as Hawk liked it best.

Hawk's hand slid down the length of bare flesh on the backless dress as he pulled her into his protective grasp, away from the boisterous crowd.

But neither Sara's beauty, nor the eye-catching dress was what made Sara so special. It was her loyalty, generous spirit, and willfulness that drew him back time and again. And Hawk so desperately wanted that Sara back. This one scared him to death. She was too quiet and secretive.

"Baby," he murmured, as the music slowed to a soft, throbbing tempo. "Talk to me. I know something's wrong."

"Roger called while you were in the shower," Sara began.

"Roger?" Hawk said, puzzled as to what Sara's brother could have said to make her like this.

"Yes. He called to wish us Happy New Year. He's been called to Washington, D.C. He hinted at changing to some supervisory position and staying out of the field. Said he didn't want anything like Levette happening again. He said Colonel Harris sends thanks, too.''

"But, Sara . . . that's good news, isn't it?''

Sara nodded her head and leaned into the curve under Hawk's chin. His arms tightened around her. He felt the rapid flight of her pulse under his fingertips as they danced. This subdued Sara was even scarier than Sara drunk.

"Come with me, sweetheart,'' Hawk whispered, and led her through the crowd to the glass-enclosed terrace that the throng of partygoers had abandoned for the dance floor.

Sara walked slowly to the edge of the terrace, secure from cold and the height behind the heavy glass walls, but they couldn't hide the magnificence nor the expanse of the Texas night sky, peppered with tiny, twinkling pinpoints of starlight.

Sensing Hawk's close scrutiny, she knew it was time to tell him and turned swiftly, suddenly anxious now that the time was here. As she turned, the hem of her dress flared out like the petals of a rose in full bloom and then fell, wrapping itself about Sara's legs like a lover's caress.

Hawk caught his breath at the picture she made, silhouetted against the night. This woman . . . his woman . . . was so beautiful and so much in his blood, he couldn't even think of why they'd come out and then he remembered.

"Sara. What is it, baby?'' his deep voice beckoned her to share. "I know you too well. There's something you're keeping from me. Please . . . are you having second thoughts about anything?''

The hesitance and fear in his voice shamed Sara into an

instant answer that reassured him, but still left him concerned for her.

"No! No!" she cried, and grabbed convulsively at his arms as they reached toward her. *They are such strong, capable, loving hands,* Sara thought, *and they hold my heart.* "I never want you to go away from me again. When you went back to the mountain with Roger, that was the hardest thing I've ever had to do . . . to let you go."

Hawk sighed and smiled, reached into his jacket pocket and set a small, black velvet box in Sara's hand. She closed her shaky fingers around it as if it would fly away if she didn't hold on tightly.

"Open it, Sara. It won't disappear," he coaxed.

Sara looked at the joy and expectation on his face and smiled tenderly as she slowly opened the lid.

Yellow fire winked back at her as the lights from the room caught in the ring's heart.

"Oh, Hawk! It's so beautiful."

Hawk took the diamond from Sara's hand and slid it gently on the third finger of her left hand.

"This just makes us official. You already have my heart, Sara Beaudry. This is for forever."

Tears welled in her eyes as Sara clasped a shaky hand to her breast, trying to slow down the erratic thump of her heart.

"Okay, sweetheart," she whispered, "now we need to talk about forever."

Hawk breathed a sigh of relief. Now, maybe he was finally going to find out what was wrong with Sara.

"We haven't had much time to discuss the mundane things that make a marriage work," Sara said, unsure which way to go with her rambling thoughts, but she had to start somewhere.

"I know that's true, baby. But if you have love, everything else kind of falls into place and what doesn't, we can throw away."

"Some things can't just be thrown away, Hawk. Some things are too precious to lose."

"Sure, honey, I didn't mean anything important. What are you getting at? Don't you trust me yet, Sara? Haven't I proven that I trust you?"

"Yes, yes," Sara muttered, tears beginning to thicken her speech. "Oh God, I'm just messing this up."

"Dammit, Sara," Hawk said as he grabbed her by the shoulders and gave her a gentle shake. "You're scaring the hell out of me."

He leaned back against the wall of the terrace and pulled Sara with him into the shadows. Maybe this feeling of panic would subside if he could just hold her.

"I'm sorry, darling," Sara said, and cupped her hand against his cheek in apology. "It's just that we haven't discussed anything," her words coming out in a rush as she continued. "We don't know where we're going to live."

Hawk sighed, knew he still wasn't to the bottom of Sara's secrecy but went along with her game for the time being.

"Well, I've installed caretakers at the cabin to look after the property and Dog, if he ever decides to come home. As far as I'm concerned, it's up to you. All I require is one redhead in residence, the location doesn't mean a damn. You're all I need to be happy."

Sara smiled as she stepped closer to Hawk, fitting herself snugly between his legs as he leaned against the shadowed walls.

"So, you think you're happy do you, Indian?" Sara

teased, and was rewarded by a look of relief appearing in the worried expression he wore.

"I know I am, baby," he said, and nuzzled through the mass of curls against her neck before he found just the spot he was searching for and took a small, sharp nip at the delicate vein that pulsed with the life he so cherished.

Sara moaned in pleasure and Hawk smiled to himself as he felt her melt against him. This was the Sara he wanted back.

"We'd better go back inside," Hawk murmured, "it's a little chilly out here and you've had a long, long day."

"Wait," Sara said, "there's something I have to tell you before we go." She sighed as she watched a tiny flicker of panic come and go in the dark green eyes she loved so much. "Sweetheart, don't you trust me yet," she coaxed, as a note of sadness came into her speech. "What I have to tell you will make you very happy. I have something to give you," Sara said, and reached down.

Hawk felt her claim his hand, raising it toward her lips, and he felt his breath catch in the back of his throat before he could manage to speak.

"I don't need anything . . . anything in this world but you, Sara," he whispered, his voice low and hoarse as his eyes devoured every nuance of her behavior.

Sara smiled that same slow, secretive smile she'd been playing with all night and raised the palm of his hand to her lips and then splayed it gently against her stomach.

"Not even your child?" she asked.

Hawk stared, transfixed at his hand on the flat of her stomach and forgot to breathe. There was something he meant to say, but it got all mixed up with the huge lump in the back of his throat. He tried to look at Sara's face, but he couldn't see it clearly through the veil of tears that came from nowhere, blinding him with an intensity he had never known.

Sweet, sweet Jesus. Sara is going to have my baby. The flood of emotion that went through him was as quick and overwhelming as the feeling he had when he made love to Sara. And they'd made love enough for a dozen babies. He'd never even thought she wasn't protected, his modern little Wildcat . . . but he was as much to blame. He had never asked and carelessness was not one of his normal traits. This lady had driven everything from his mind and installed herself firmly in his heart. And now this . . .

Sara's heart melted. She saw the emotion Hawk battled as he tried to speak and his silence said more than his words ever could.

Hawk cupped his hands on either side of her face, tilted her head back, looked straight into her eyes, brimming with so much love for him, and saw immortality.

"A baby . . . you're going to have my baby . . ."

But he never finished his sentence as Sara felt herself go airborn. Hawk had her safe in his arms, whirling her around and around inside the walls of the crystal-covered terrace, until the stars overhead all melted into one huge, sparkling ball of light.

The air was filled with the old familiar strains of "Auld Lang Syne," but it was the beautiful sound of Hawk's joyful laughter that Sara would always remember.

"I love you, too," Sara said teasingly, when Hawk finally came to his senses enough to put her feet back on solid ground.

"Happy New Year, little Wildcat," Hawk whispered through the din of the merrymakers that began spilling back out onto the terrace.

But Sara heard him loud and clear.

"Happy New Year, my love," she answered, "all the rest of our lives."

EPILOGUE

"Oh God! Oh God, another one." Sara moaned as she leaned her swollen body back against the seat of the Wildcat and allowed the contraction to take control of her sanity.

"They're only four minutes apart. Dammit, Sara, do you have to be in a hurry about everything?"

Outwardly Hawk was calm and teasing, as he pushed the gas pedal all the way to the floor. Inside, however, he was a wreck. He felt Sara's grip on his arm as he maneuvered through the ever-present traffic of Dallas, Texas.

The contractions must be getting unbearable for her. He could tell by the way she clung to him when they took possession of her body. He'd never been so worried. If a miracle didn't occur, he wasn't going to make it to the hospital in time.

Then, as if in answer to his prayer, his miracle appeared in the rearview mirror of the Wildcat—flashing red lights, siren and all.

"Thank God," Hawk muttered, and reached over and

patted Sara's swollen tummy. "For once, an Indian is glad to see the cavalry on the horizon."

Sara's giggle choked in her throat as another fierce contraction nearly lifted her from the seat.

Hawk took one frantic look at Sara, slowed down and motioned for the policeman to come alongside.

The policeman took one look at the anxious expression on Hawk's face and the pain on Sara's, and led the way to Dallas Memorial.

In less time than he could ever have hoped, they were at the emergency entrance. The policeman stopped his patrol car a few feet in front of the Wildcat as it came to a sudden stop by the wide, glass entryway to the emergency room. He was out of his patrol car and holding the door to the red sportscar open almost before it came to a complete stop.

"Thanks for the help," Hawk said, carefully lifting Sara into his arms. "We couldn't have made it without you."

"My pleasure," the policeman grinned, "and good luck, too." He watched the big man disappear inside Dallas Memorial with his precious cargo. It was incidents like this one that made the rest of his job bearable.

"It hurts so much," Sara moaned. Her bottom lip was bruised and bleeding. She'd bitten down once too many times to keep from crying aloud. Sara Hawk had reached the limit of her pain tolerance.

She knew she was heavy, but there was no way on earth she could stand, and Hawk wasn't putting her down. She could tell that by the look in his eyes and the expression of concern on his face.

"Hawk, please. I need . . ." and then her plea was cut short, as she let the tearing pain float her away.

"I know, baby. I know. I'm sorry, Sara. We're almost there. Just hang in a little longer for me, love, for me."

"Lady! I need help," Hawk cried, as he rushed up to the receptionist behind the desk of emergency admitting.

"Yes, sir. Just put her in one of those wheelchairs." She pointed toward the wall behind Hawk. "I need you to fill out these papers. A doctor will see you shortly."

Sara wrapped her arm around Hawk's shoulder as the woman spoke and buried her face in his neck. Her cheeks were wet from tears and perspiration, as she struggled to maintain what was left of her sanity in this public place. Actually, all she wanted to do was find a dark, private hole and let the pain take her away. She couldn't fight it much longer. Then, another contraction, even closer than the one before, tore a scream from the depths of her soul and Hawk flew into a rage.

"Lady," he said coldly, "I'm not putting my wife in any damn chair. She couldn't sit up if I did. Look at her, dammit!"

"Oh my!" she muttered, "it's you again."

She recognized Sara and the big man carrying her. She should. They had given her nightmares for weeks after her last encounter.

Hawk was too rattled to realize what the lady meant. He just wanted action. "This is my wife. And she's about to give birth to our child, and if she has one more damn contraction in this waiting room while I'm holding her, you're going to . . ."

"I know, I know," the lady interrupted, as she dashed down the hall, calling for her helper to notify the labor room. "I'm going to be eating my food through a straw for the rest of my days . . . or something like that."

Hawk took a good look at the lady's horrified face and another at Sara's weak grin.

"That's right!" he laughed as he followed the panicky woman down the hall. "We've been here before, haven't we, little Wildcat?"

"Mr. Hawk," the doctor said, handing the tiny, squirming bundle into Hawk's outstretched arms. "Meet your son, all nine pounds of him."

Hawk had never left Sara's side. He'd been with her through every step of the delivery and in that short time, he had never been so scared, or so proud, as he witnessed Sara's suffering. And all for him . . . and their baby.

Sara smiled through tears of relief and joy as she watched her husband hold their son for the first time.

Hawk clasped the baby carefully against his chest and looked in wonder at the tiny but perfect product of his and Sara's love. He was a fine son, perfectly formed with all the necessary fingers and toes. Hawk gently touched the mane of damp, black curls on the baby's tiny head. The hair was so soft.

"He isn't crying," Hawk worried. "I thought babies cried when they were born."

"Maybe this one doesn't have anything to cry about, sweetheart," Sara whispered.

The baby squirmed and worked his tiny mouth toward Hawk's finger as Hawk stroked the side of his son's face.

"I don't think my finger is going to do you any good, little one," Hawk chuckled, as he walked toward Sara.

The baby's tiny eyelids squinched and blinked as his unfocused gaze turned bright, green eyes toward the deep, husky voice and the strong arms holding him so tenderly.

"He knows your voice, Hawk," Sara said.

"He should," Hawk answered, and touched the petal soft cheek of the baby with his lips. "I've talked to you every night before we slept, haven't I, son?"

Sara looked into Hawk's eyes. The jade brimmed with unshed tears as he carefully leaned over and brushed Sara's weary mouth with his lips.

"Thank you, Sara. Thank you for my son . . . and for being the best thing in my life."

Sara watched Mackenzie Hawk cradling their son in his arms.

So beautiful and so strong, my guardian angel. Thank God when he fell to earth, he fell into my arms, Sara thought.

And Sara knew, as fatigue overwhelmed her, that he would watch over their son, Beaudry Hawk, as carefully as he had watched over her.

She closed her eyes and smiled as she drifted off to sleep, receiving Hawk's tribute and his tender kiss as her due. She was tired but at peace. Sara Beaudry had done her part in bringing Mackenzie Hawk full circle. Now, as Sara Hawk, she could know the joy of watching their child grow to manhood, as Old Woman had watched Hawk, many years ago on the Kiamichi.

SHARE THE FUN . . .
SHARE YOUR NEW-FOUND TREASURE!!

You don't want to let your new books out of your sight? That's okay. Your friends can get their own. Order below.

No. 1 ALWAYS by Catherine Sellers
A modern day "knight in shining armor." Forever . . . for always!

No. 2 NO HIDING PLACE by Brooke Sinclair
Pretty government agent & handsome professor = mystery & romance.

No. 3 SOUTHERN HOSPITALITY by Sally Falcon
North meets South. War is declared. Both sides win!!!

No. 4 WINTERFIRE by Lois Faye Dyer
Beautiful NY model and rugged Idaho rancher find their own magic.

No. 5 A LITTLE INCONVENIENCE by Judy Christenberry
Liz faces every obstacle Jason throws at her—even his love.

No. 6 CHANGE OF PACE by Sharon Brondos
Can Sam protect himself from Deirdre, the green-eyed temptress?

No. 21 THAT JAMES BOY by Lois Faye Dyer
Jesse believes in love at first sight. Will he convince Sarah?

No. 22 NEVER LET GO by Laura Phillips
Ryan has a big dilemma. Kelly is the answer to *all* his prayers.

No. 23 A PERFECT MATCH by Susan Combs
Ross can keep Emily safe but can he save himself from Emily?

No. 24 REMEMBER MY LOVE by Pamela Macaluso
Will Max ever remember the special love he and Deanna shared?

No. 25 LOVE WITH INTEREST by Darcy Rice
Stephanie & Elliot find $47,000,000 *plus* interest—true love!

No. 26 NEVER A BRIDE by Leanne Banks
The last thing Cassie wanted was a relationship. Joshua had other ideas.

No. 27 GOLDILOCKS by Judy Christenberry
David and Susan join forces and get tangled in their own web.

No. 28 SEASON OF THE HEART by Ann Hammond
Can Lane and Maggie's newfound feelings stand the test of time?

No. 29 FOSTER LOVE by Janis Reams Hudson
Morgan comes home to claim his children but Sarah claims his heart.

No. 30 REMEMBER THE NIGHT by Sally Falcon
Joanna throws caution to the wind. Is Nathan fantasy or reality?